A Steamy Romance Adventure

By Tamara Eastlick

You ARE Strong!
Enjoy!
♡ Tamara Eastlick

1

Table of Contents

Copyright ©2021 by Tamara Eastlick

This book is dedicated to:

My Grandma

Betty Lou Goree Hildebrand

who inspired in me, a love for stories and storytelling.

Prologue

All she could hear was her labored breathing and the pounding of her heart. Running, she ducked into the alley and ran to the nearby dumpster. Crouching down, she took a minute to try and catch her breath. Touching her eye, she winced. That will be black and purple tomorrow for sure. She gingerly ran her tongue along the inside of her lip and winced again. He got her good this time.

Watching the entrance of the alley Ericka leaned back against the building. Taking a deep breath to try and calm her heart, she caught a whiff of the dumpster and wrinkled her nose. Looking down she grabbed her bag and did a quick inventory of what she had. She learned long ago to keep an emergency bag, or GO bag as she called it. Inside she found a couple outfits, a pair of tennis shoes, some snacks, a jacket, a wig, an unlisted cell phone and money. Counting her money, she checked to see how much she had on hand. Getting her things later will be a bit harder but she knew a few people who would help. Chad will for sure have someone watching her apartment now.

Inventory made; she closed her eyes for a second trying to formulate a plan. It was time to relocate; again.

Too bad, because she was really liking this place. She had grown lazy and tonight showed it. It had been a close call; closer than she liked. She needed to figure out where to go and what to do. She could travel under a fake name; she had done it before. It was the starting over part that made things hard. She was so lucky to have her support group. She had a chain of contacts that will be able to help her get settled. She needed to call Grace and let her know the emergency plan had been activated. She just had to pick a new location. She thought she could blend in and lose herself in New York, but she underestimated him yet again.

Staying in the shadows, she made her way, as quietly as possible, to the end of the alley. Throwing her back pack on, she checked the street to make sure there was no one searching for her. He was probably still unconscious, but she had to plan for the unexpected. She needed to get to the train station and get a ticket out of town. Walking away, she dialed Grace's number.

"Hello" Grace said.

"Grace, it's Ericka. I've had to activate my emergency plan." She whispered into the phone.

"Oh no, are you ok? How bad are you hurt?" She asked quietly.

9

"Not bad this time, but he is knocked out in my apartment. You still have a key right?" Ericka asked.

"Yes, I will have the guys from the shelter come with me and we will pack up your things. Do you know where you are going yet?" She questioned.

"No, just getting out of town tonight. I will make a better plan after I am safe and have had some rest."

"I'm not going to ask where you are, but I want to make sure you have access to what you need." She sighed.

"I am close to where I need to go. I am ok for now. I will contact you when I have settled. I may need you to help me with a local chapter, I will need to make an emergency plan when I get settled." Ericka replied.

"Of course, we will get you sorted out. Please be careful and watch your back." Grace said.

"I will. Thank you for everything. You have been a true friend. I'll talk to you soon. Bye." Ericka whispered and hung up.

Ericka put the phone away and turned toward the sound of footsteps behind her. Turning back around, she found she was almost to Grand Central Station. She just needed to get there; then she could blend in with the crowds.

Maybe if she was lucky there will be a group of people to help her disappear. Picking up her pace, she turned the corner, there was Grand Central Station. Running up the steps she ran in, straight to the bathroom. She needed to clean up her face and put on her wig and jacket. It had been a while since she had to disappear but these survival instincts never went away. Fight or Flight. Tonight, it had been a bit of both. Getting into a stall she took a moment to just breathe. Closing her eyes, she replayed the last couple hours in her mind.

She had been expecting her take out order, so when there was a knock at the door, she didn't ask who it was. Something she had learned to do over the years. She had gotten lazy. She opened the door and saw him standing there. She tried to shut the door, but as usual he was too strong for her.

She backed up toward the kitchen. She needed something she could defend herself with. "What are you doing here," she asked.

"What do you think Annie. I have come for you. You made it extra hard for me this time, Ericka." He snorted with derision.

"I still have a restraining order against you Chad. You need to leave or I will call 911." She said while easing

11

her way toward the kitchen. She could get out of her apartment via her fire escape. She needed to think and remember her plan.

"I am your husband, Annie. I don't care if you get a hundred restraining orders or change your name. You are mine." He growled.

"We are no longer married Chad and you know it. You need to get help." She spat out.

"I will always come for you Annie." And he lunged for her. Catching her wrist, he yanked her hard, up against his body. She fought him. Kicking his shins and trying to knee his groin. But all she was doing was making him madder. She didn't even see the first punch coming. He caught her lip and her knees buckled. Struggling to get up she used her free hand to grasp at something to help. He was pulling her toward the bedroom now and she knew if she didn't get free things would go from bad to worse. She grabbed for a vase that was on the end table but couldn't quite reach it. He was struggling to get her to go with him and swung again, catching her eye. She must have blacked out because the next thing she knew she was laying on the couch. She slowly opened her eyes to see if she could see him. There was no sign of him but she heard a noise coming from the hallway. She quietly rolled off the couch to her hands and knees. She was almost to the door when he came back in.

"Where the hell do you think you are going?" He yelled.

Jumping to her feet she grabbed the vase and as he came at her she swung and smashed it on his head. Thank goodness he went down. She ran to the closet and grabbed her go bag and got the hell out of there.

Hearing a stall door shut, snapped Ericka to attention and to her current problem. She put her wig and jacket on. She needed to clean her lip and then find the ticket booth. Coming out of the stall she looked both ways. She wouldn't put it past Chad to come into the ladies' restroom looking for her. She had already stayed in there too long. Washing her hands, she grabbed a few towels and wet them to clean her face. A lady in her late 30's, early 40's came out of a stall and to the sinks. Ericka kept her face down trying to hide her face.

"Are you ok dear?" she asked Ericka.

"I will be. Thank you for asking." She responded.

"Do you need help? My husband and I are headed to Atlanta. You are welcome to travel with us." She said, gently.

Ericka looked up and into the mirror, locking eyes with the lady. She saw compassion and, surprisingly, understanding in her gaze. *"I'm not sure."* Ericka was wary but still wanted to disappear and this might be her best bet.

"Well, we are sitting by Track 112 if you decide to join us. My name is Mary and my husband is George." She turned to leave and stopped, *"You missed a few locks of your hair in the back dear. Make sure you get all your hair tucked up inside the wig. And take these."* She handed Ericka a pair of sunglasses. *"I don't have much for the lip but I can help hide your eye."*

Ericka just stared at the glasses then looked up as the door was closing. She fixed her hair in the back, washed her lip and put on the sunglasses. Ericka made a decision right then that she was going to trust Mary. She hadn't had to do anything, but she had reached out, and she could use all the help she could get right now.

She tried to catch up to Mary but didn't see her in the sea of people. It was her turn to disappear now and she lost herself in the same sea of people, searching for Mary. Making her way to the track she was alert and on edge. She didn't see Mary but felt a hand on her shoulder making her jump. *"I'm sorry, I didn't mean to scare you."* Mary said.

"Have you changed your mind?" She gestured to a gentleman by the ticket booth.

"Please. I just need to get out of here." Ericka whispered. "If you don't mind if I ride along with you, I would appreciate it. Atlanta is not my final stop but it's on the way."

Mary smiled. "Of course, you are welcome to join us. Let's get you a ticket. It will be safer if you are not by yourself."

Ericka turned with Mary and walked to the ticket counter. Getting her tickets, she joined George and Mary at the platform. The first train was leaving in 30 minutes. Mary turned to Ericka and said, "Let me introduce you to George. This is my husband. And what is your name dear?"

"My name is Grace." Ericka responded. "Thank you for helping me."

Mary patted her hand and said, "I have been here before my dear and I only wish I would have had someone reach out to me."

Ericka looked quickly at George, who smiled. "Don't you worry about George. He is the one who saved me." Mary said smiling at George.

Ericka tried to smile and ended up grimacing. "Don't you worry about a thing, Miss. We will keep you safe." George said.

Nodding to him, she looked around checking faces to make sure she didn't see Chad. Mary took her arm and guided her closer to the train. They would be boarding soon. George stood on Ericka's other side and for the first time in hours she felt hope.

Chapter 1

Ericka woke with a start. She had been having these same dreams for days now and she knew that they were warnings. She just wasn't sure if it was Chad or something else. She sat up and surveyed her surroundings. She was at home, in her apartment, in Los Angeles. It had been a while since she had thought about Mary and George. She should reach out and let them know she was still safe.

These dreams were bringing back lots of old memories; some good, some not so good. Traveling with Mary and George to Atlanta had been a blessing. She was able to get some much-needed rest so she could come up with a game plan on what to do next. Mary and George even opened their house to Ericka for a few days just to put time and distance between Ericka and Chad. Mary never went into detail about her experience, but she knew George loved her and protected her fiercely. They worked with an outreach program to help other people like Ericka who were struggling with abuse.

Getting up, she stretched and got ready for her day. Today was extra special. She was graduating from college with her degree in business. This was a huge accomplishment for several reasons but mainly that she was able to stay in one location long enough to accomplish it. She had taken classes on and off but to be able to actually graduate was amazing. It had been years since she had heard anything about Chad. Shaking her head, she needed to push thoughts of Chad and her dreams aside.

Today was graduation and in a couple days she was flying up to Oregon. She was looking forward to it, and the trip from Oregon to visit Jemma and Rob on the island. Jemma was one of her past roommates and best friend. She met Jemma soon after coming to Los Angeles. Ericka had seen her walking around the campus and noticed the signs of abuse. Ericka befriended Jemma and was able to direct her to the help and support she needed. She had been her sponsor of sorts and helped her when needed. The last time she had to pick her up from the hospital, it had been the worst she had seen. Luckily, she was able to help get Jemma's mom here to take her home to Oregon. She was safe now and in a loving marriage with Rob and they lived on the big island of Hawaii. She loved Jemma and her family. The Morgan family were special and ever since she reached out and helped Jemma, the family had adopted Ericka.

Later this month she was supposed to meet Jemma and Rob in Oregon for a family reunion. She was very much looking forward to this but was concerned about her dreams. She had been having repeat dreams and that never boded well.

Ericka had been blessed with a gift of sorts. It was not always accurate, and it was sometimes hard to determine if it was foresight or if it was what she was wanting. But her gift had been right more than wrong, for the better part of her adult life. Now that she knew what clues to look for it was easier to spot. It was also easier to see things for others more than herself. Crazy how that works.

She needed to take this one day at a time, and today was all about her graduation. She pushed those thoughts aside and went on about her day. She was looking forward to graduation. This was a huge accomplishment for her considering all she had gone through. Now that school was done though she needed to look forward and see what her next step should be. But she would give herself time to enjoy the Morgan reunion and then try to figure everything out.

*   *   *   *   *   *   *   *

Steven was cranky. There was no other word for it. Ok maybe hangry might be more appropriate. He just wasn't a morning person and he had taken a very early flight. He had been visiting Jemma and Rob in Hawaii. Now though he was stuck in Los Angeles due to his flight being cancelled. The next direct flight wasn't until 9pm, so here he was stuck in Los Angeles. He knew that Jemma was flying in today to surprise her best friend Ericka, who was graduating. Then everyone would fly home to Oregon for the reunion. He needed to make a decision on if he should just wait and book his flight out with everyone else or not.

After dealing with the booking agents, he determined it would be easier just to wait for everyone else. He wasn't in a rush to get home. He decided to call Jemma, "Hey when does your flight get into LA?" he asked.

"Well, we are at the airport now and I am supposed to be in sometime this afternoon. Why what's happening?" Jemma asked.

"My flight got cancelled so I'm just going to wait and head home with you guys, but I didn't know if I should stay here at the airport or head to Ericka's." He questioned.

"Just go to Ericka's, I'm sure she is just getting ready for today. Rob and the kids are flying out tomorrow. And coming to Ericka's house for a few days before we head up to mom and dads." Pausing she said, "You have her address, right?" She questioned

"Yes," Steven confirmed. "I'll head there now. She will just get two surprises today."

Grabbing his suitcase from baggage claim he headed out to grab a taxi to head to Ericka's place. He had been there before when Jemma lived with her. He wondered if she would be ok with having him just stop by. He knew a little of her history but not everything. He knew she helped Jemma with that ass, Clint, and she had alluded to having gone through something similar. Looking out the window he thought about Ericka. He had always loved being in her company. She was funny, smart and not to mention good looking. They were good friends, but he was also the brother of her best friend, which was an awkward place to be. He couldn't ever remember her talking about a relationship or special someone in her life.

Steven could relate. It had been some time since he had been in a serious relationship. But none of his relationships lasted longer than a few months. Steven was lucky to have been able to start up a dot com company right out of college in Portland, which demanded a lot of his time. He recently sold his company and was on a quest to find himself. He needed something to do. He just felt like he was treading water and the current was taking him on a ride. He never knew if it would be rapids ahead or a calm current.

Pulling up to the apartment complex, he got his bags & paid the cabbie. Looking up he saw her apartment and saw movement in the window. Well at least someone is home he thought to himself. Gathering his courage, he started up the stairs. Knocking on her door he heard her ask who it was. He smiled. "It's Steven. Steven Morgan." He heard her gasp while fumbling with the locks on the door. Did she really have 4 locks, no 5 locks on her door? He made note to take a look at her door later.

Throwing open the door, Ericka appeared. She was so beautiful with her chestnut-colored hair and bright blue eyes. Every time he saw her, his stomach flipped. But she was his sister's best friend.

She smiled so big you could see her dimple in her right cheek. "Steven!! Oh, my goodness!! You were the last person I expected to see today. What are you doing here? Is everything ok?" she asked while grabbing his hand and pulling him into the apartment and giving him a big hug.

Oh, he loved her hugs. She always seems to make people feel special. Today though, there was an electric current that ran through his body. He pulled back from her a bit; partly out of shock and partly to answer her question, he said, "My flight got cancelled and I didn't want to wait 12 hours at the airport, so I thought I'd come and see you." She looked at him and smiled. He said, "Although a little birdie told me that you were graduating today and I thought maybe I could be a cheerleader for you today."

"Are you kidding? I would love that." Walking toward the kitchen she asked, "When do you fly back out?"

"I don't know, I haven't scheduled it yet, but the next flight north isn't 'til late this evening. I was thinking though maybe I would just wait and see when you are heading up for the Morgan reunion, and I could just fly up with you." He replied.

"That would be great. I really do hate traveling alone." Now in the kitchen she stopped at the fridge and asked, "Have you eaten yet?"

He laughed, "No and I'm so hungry I could probably clear out your fridge. Why don't I take you to breakfast? Isn't there a little café around the corner?"

Shutting the door, she looked up and exclaimed "Deal! Let me grab my purse." And they were off.

Walking toward the café, they were chatting a mile, a minute, like they normally did when together. It was funny that she was Jemma's best friend but in an odd way was his as well. He was in contact more with Ericka than any other person, not counting his family of course. She was the easiest person to talk to, and she genuinely wanted to hear what you had to say. He was silently thanking the powers that be, for cancelling his flight. He needed to talk out what he was going to do and Ericka was the best person he knew for this discussion.

Once seated at the café, Ericka turned to Steven, "So what have you been up to? I know you were at Jemma's, but what are your plans now that the company has sold? Any new ventures catch your eye?"

Taking a drink of his coffee, he shook his head. "I have no idea what I'm going to do now. I was hoping that being at Jemma's would help me clear my head but I still feel like I'm wandering with no destination. Does that even make sense?"

Ericka smiled at him. The smile that always made his stomach flip. "I know exactly how you feel. Today I graduate from college and I have no idea what I'm going to do. I am just taking things a day at a time right now until after my trips I have planned."

Their food arrived and they chatted while eating. Before they knew it, the time had flown and it was time for Ericka to start getting ready for her graduation. Steven loved the fact that he got to be here for her special day. He couldn't wait to see her face when Jemma arrived though.

She was going to be super surprised when Jemma showed up in an hour or two.

Back at the house Ericka showed Steven the spare room he could stay in and use to change and told him to make himself at home while she got ready. Steven threw his bags on the bed and went to head back out to the living room and walked by a door that was partially open. He remembered this place had Jack and Jill bathrooms and as he reached to shut it, he looked up and caught the reflection of Ericka in the bathroom mirror. She was just stepping into the shower. He could not look away from the vision Ericka made. As she shut the curtain, she turned and looked in the mirror and they locked eyes. "Sorry it was open. I'll see you in a bit." Steven said awkwardly.

Shutting the door quickly, he leaned against it. Closing his eyes, he pictured her just like she had been moments ago. Shaking his head and opening his eyes he walked down the hall to the living room to wait for Jemma to arrive.

* * * * * * * *

Ericka smiled to herself. Did she just catch Steven peeking on her? It had been sometime since she had a roommate so she always left the doors open. When she looked in the mirror and locked eyes with Steven, the air

25

seemed to sizzle. But then he stammered, blushed and made a hasty retreat. You would think he was a teenager the way he acted when caught. But truth be told they were only a couple years apart in age.

Ericka had always found Steven to be so easy going and such a great friend. Jemma and Steven were her best friends. Although only Jemma knew the painful details about her ex-husband. She knew that she should tell Steven and that he probably had a good idea of what happened just from conversations, but she felt with these reoccurring dreams she needed to trust him fully and tell him the story.

Finishing her shower, she pushed those thoughts aside and concentrated on graduation. She was just finishing pulling on her summer dress when there was a knock at the front door. Ericka turned to her bedroom door and with a towel on her head she went to the living room. Wanting to know who was at the door, she went to Steven and just as he closed the door and turned to Ericka with a big grin, he stepped aside and there was Jemma! Squealing and throwing her towel, she ran to Jemma and wrapped her in her arms. Tears streaming down her face, she pulled back and said "I thought you couldn't make it. Oh, my goodness, this is the best surprise."

A cough sounded from her right and she turned and looked at Steven, "Ok one of the best surprises today."

Steven grinned and nodded saying, "I thought that is what you said. Do carry on."

Ericka smacked his shoulder and pulled both her favorite people into a group hug. "My two most favorite people in the whole world will be here on my very special day. I couldn't ask for more."

Crying Jemma said, "You know hard it was to keep it a secret? I've been planning this for weeks. Steven just got lucky."

They all laughed and walked into the living room. Steven took Jemma's bags into her room. Ericka turned to Jemma, "What about the kids and Rob? Are they meeting you in Oregon?"

Jemma smiled. "No, they fly in to LAX tomorrow. You will have a full house for a couple days and we will all head north together."

Ericka continued crying. Her family was here. She couldn't be happier at this moment. Then Chad's face popped into her mind. She stilled. Jemma, knowing Ericka so well stopped, "What is it?"

Ericka didn't want to ruin this day so she pushed the image of Chad aside and shook her head. "I'm just overwhelmed with happiness. Like Birdie's Momma says, in Hope Floats, 'My cup runneth over'. Thank you for making this day even more special."

Jemma smiled, "I know what you have had to overcome to make it this far. I am so proud of you and I cannot wait to celebrate you."

Steven walked back in, "Celebrate? Did you bring the air horn?"

Jemma and Ericka both groaned together. "No." they both said at the same time. And all three started laughing.

The rest of the afternoon flew by. Getting to the college and finding seat was super fun, but Ericka was glad that Jemma was here with Steven. She couldn't believe that they were here for her.

The ceremony droned on and on but finally it was time for her to walk across the stage. She got her diploma with her two best friends cheering her on from the audience. Smiling at the crowd, she went and sat back down. Today had been one of the best days. She was so happy at this moment in time.

*　　*　　*　　*　　*　　*　　*　　*

There was a slight breeze as he watched Annie walk across the stage with that grin on her face. Finding her this time had been harder, a lot harder. Luckily for him, she hadn't changed her name a second time. It had taken him a long time to track her to Los Angeles, and even longer to find her in the city. He had been following her for the past week or so though. He wasn't going to storm in like last time. He was watching so he knew when to make his move.

Today he had almost blown his cover. When that guy showed up at her door and she hugged him right there for anyone to see, like a brazen hussy, he'd almost jumped out of the truck he'd been living in and stormed her apartment. Luckily for Annie, that girl showed up. As he watched the same man and woman now, at Annie's graduation, he could see this was going to take some more planning. Those bags they had didn't look like they were going anywhere any time soon. He turned back to Annie and watched as she walked back to her chair. His Annie, not Ericka whatever they called her, he would make sure that got fixed right away. She had been his Annie and he would get her back one way or another.

Finally, as the ceremony ended, he was able to get a better look at Annie. She was as beautiful as ever, but tonight she glowed. Her smile was a light in his otherwise dark and dreary existence. Why was she so happy? It was only a piece of paper after all. She had never voiced her desire to go to school. She had been content to stay home and take care of him, like he wanted. It had been a long time since he had seen that smile though and he couldn't look away. He had been watching her for almost a week now and she had never been this happy. What was she looking at that was causing that smile? It had better not be because of that guy. He watched as Annie joined them in the stands, hugging each other. The guy held on to her a little too long. He needed to nip that in the bud. He watched as they made their way out to the parking lot. Chad followed close enough to see what they were doing but not too close to be spotted. As they got to the car and all started to get in, Annie paused and looked up. Looking around she frowned but got into her car. He smiled. *She knew that I was here and watching.* Annie had always been able to know things. She must be able to sense him.

Walking to his truck his mind drifted back to the last time he had seen her. *It was the night in New York where she had caught him off guard with that vase. When he came too there were police all around and he was being loaded onto a gurney. He couldn't see Annie so he kept asking where his wife was and no one knew what he was talking about. At the hospital that stupid police officer started to read him his rights because they found the restraining order that Annie, no, Ericka had on him and that the apartment was hers and not his. They had a guard at the door, but they couldn't take him in until he was discharged. He had to get 12 stitches and be observed overnight due to a concussion. All that had kept him going was the fact that he was going to enjoy getting back at Annie for those stitches. This was the first time she had injured him in all the years he had known her.*

It was after midnight when the guard decided to go grab some coffee and it was then that Chad had been able to sneak out of his hospital bed. He wasn't sure what he was going to do but he knew he had to lay low for a while. After a few days he traced Annie to Grand Central Station but from there he wasn't able to track her. He had to give her credit though, she had gotten better at this evasion stuff. He watched her apartment for a few days but when those two big guys and that tiny woman showed up with boxes, he knew Annie was on the run. He decided to head home to regroup. He was going to have to bide his time again so he could work enough to get the funds and time off to find her. But he would find her.

Chad snapped out of his memory and drove back to Annie's place. He had all the time in the world now that he no longer had to deal with that stupid job. But he had to

31

watch and see what happened now that she had people with her. He should have made his move two days ago when she had been walking back from the store. He had been following her on foot and he thought she had seen him, but she never turned around. He should have gone with his gut and just snatched her up then and there. Now things have gotten more complicated. He needed to think this through and watch patiently for his time to strike. And that was one thing he was good at, waiting and watching.

Chapter 2

Walking to the car tonight the hair on the back of Erica's neck stood on end. She felt eyes watching her but couldn't see anyone staring at her. She knew she was being jumpy because of the dreams. She decided to push those thoughts aside and enjoy her friends and her success. They went to dinner and then back to her place. She was so happy both of them would be staying. It was just after 11 o'clock when Jemma said she was done and needed to get up early to get Rob and the kids anyway. She hugged Ericka and kissed Steven's cheek.

Steven sat on the couch while Ericka was sitting on the floor with the couch as her back rest. They were just talking about everything and anything when Steven cleared his throat and said, "Ericka, I wanted to apologize for earlier today. I really was just shutting the door when you saw me. I wanted to make sure you knew I wasn't standing there the whole time watching you."

Ericka laughed, "Don't worry about it. Being alone all the time, I forget about things like doors every now and again." Nudging his leg with her shoulder she teased, "You were so cute being embarrassed like that. I don't think I've ever seen you blush like that before."

Steven smiled, "Yes well, you would have blushed too had the roles been reversed."

Ericka stood and walked toward the kitchen, "Oh I don't know about that. I probably would have stood there a bit longer." She said over her shoulder.

*   *   *   *   *   *   *   *

Steven blushed again. What the hell was wrong with him. He wasn't some immature virgin. But talking to Ericka about this certainly brought that guy out. He watched Ericka clean up after the day and wondered how it might be to have this all the time. That was a thought he didn't want to examine too closely. He was just lonely. He hadn't had a girlfriend in quite a while. He was just feeling the loneliness more acutely with being with Ericka and Jemma both. He just needed a good nights' rest. He stood and walked to the kitchen, "I think I'm going to call it a night as well, that is unless you need me for anything."

Ericka turned around and the corners of her lips slowly raised into a smile. "What?" he asked.

Ericka laughed, "Oh nothing, it's just no one has offered their help in a long time."

34

Steven thought about what he said and the inuendo he had let slip. He smiled and shook his head. "Where is your head tonight? I hope it's a gutter that is at least close by."

*   *   *   *   *   *   *   *

Ericka's laugh came from her toes. She was having the best night and she loved this playful teasing she and Steven had progressed to. She wondered what it meant for them down the road. She hoped that things wouldn't get too awkward. With that thought in her mind she threw the towel at him, "I'm throwing in the towel. You won this round my friend." Still laughing at her own joke, she walked to the front door and locked all her locks.

"Can I ask you about those locks Ericka? Are you in some kind of trouble? That's some serious security." Steven asked.

As much as Ericka wanted to tell Steven the whole story, now just was not the time. It had been such a great night she didn't want it to end on a sad and depressing note. "I promise to tell you soon. Just not tonight alright?" She promised.

"Ok. Just know I am here and will help you with anything you need." He vowed.

Ericka walked to him and went to kiss his cheek at the same time he turned to kiss hers. It ended in an almost kiss on the lips. They both laughed and headed to their rooms. It was late and quiet, kind of like the calm before the storm.

The next morning brought the storm. There was a flurry of activity as everyone prepared for Rob and the kids' arrival. Ericka could not wait to see Erin. She hadn't seen her since she was born and she was already getting so big. Steven got regulated to the couch as the kids would need his room. Although Charlie would probably sleep in the living room with him, if Ericka had any guesses.

She was loving having them all here and to finally be able to relax. School was done and the Morgan reunion was coming up and now she had a house full of guests that she would be able to spoil and take to her favorite places. Only thing nagging her in the back of her mind was the feeling she had at graduation last night. But she didn't have time to examine that feeling today. Besides she was able to help others but her insight into her own life had been notoriously flawed up until now. It really was hard to distinguish between what she wanted to happen and what was more than likely going to happen.

*   *   *   *   *   *   *   *

Steven took Ericka's car and headed to the airport. He thought he'd give the ladies time alone before the circus arrived, because then there would be no peace. Besides he needed to think. He was having crazy feelings and ideas popping into his brain. He was not sure how to proceed. Last night he had come awfully close to kissing Ericka. They had been flirting all day and last night he could tell something was on her mind. He just didn't know if it was him or something else. He needed to decide if he wanted to cross the friend line into relationship zone. He wanted her, but not if it was just for a quick tumble, he didn't want to cross the line just for that. Deep down he knew if they crossed that line and it went badly things would be awkward at gatherings and who knows if she would even keep coming at that point. Oh, but if they crossed that line and it went great?! How amazing would it be to finally be in a relationship with someone who knew the real him and understood him the way Ericka did. She was just as lonely as he was and they really did make a great team.

Pulling up to airport arrivals, he had to laugh at the site of Rob and the kids on the sidewalk. When he pulled up in front of them Tom was jumping up and down with Charlie's hand on his shoulder. He was a little bundle of energy. Steven hopped out and helped Rob with their luggage while Charlie helped get Erin situated in the car with the boys. All loaded up they headed out to Ericka's. Tom filled Steven in on all the excitement of flying and what had been happening since he had left, a day ago. Chuckling to himself he turned to Rob and asked, "He is very excited, huh?"

Rob laughed. "Believe it or not this is actually more subdued than he is normally. He has been working on controlling himself better. Although I think we may need another lesson or two."

Steven laughed and said, "Hey you mind if I ask you a question about Jemma?"

Rob turned and looked at Steven, "What's up?"

Steven wasn't sure how to start. "Well maybe this isn't the best time." He looked in the rearview mirror and saw the boys watching at him. "It's nothing important just a dating question." He responded.

Rob nodded and turned back to the window. "We will have a chat later. But you know our relationship was not the normal one that most people have." He laughed and shook his head. "I wouldn't trade her for anything even with all the unpleasantness that happened. No matter what you are wondering, you should think about this question. 'Would I fight to keep that person in your life.' Once you know the answer to that everything else will click into place."

"Thanks. That is something I need to think about. But I'm just not sure the next step. But we can talk more later." He said as he pulled off the freeway to head to Ericka's house.

Pulling up to the apartment, Jemma ran down the stairs and straight into Rob's arms. She kissed him long and hard in front of everyone. Rob picked her up and kissed her just as passionately as Jemma had. Steven started chuckling and looked up the stairs to see Ericka coming down and laughing at them too. "Get a room." She said laughing.

Jemma pulled back from Rob and said, "I have one thank you." She laughed and Rob put her down. The boys started filing out of the car and ran to Jemma. Rob cupped her cheek and kissed her forehead. Rob turned and unhooked Erin's car seat and handed her over to Jemma.

"Let's get your bags and head inside." Ericka said placing a hand on Steven's arm and walking toward the back of the car.

Rob must have seen the contact as his eyebrow went up to his hair line and looked at Steven. Steven smiled sheepishly and followed Ericka. Chuckling to himself, Rob and Charlie joined them at the trunk and gathered everything and started up the stairs. About halfway up Ericka stopped and turned around. Looking around the parking lot and at the apartments nearby. Steven was behind her so he too stopped and looked around wondering what she was looking for. "Is everything ok? Did we forget something?" He asked.

Shaking herself she looked into Steven's eyes. His breath caught in his throat, he could see fear and worry reflected back at him. He set the bag down and grabbed her hand. "What is it?"

Trembling she said, "I don't know for sure. But I felt the same feeling yesterday after graduation." Biting her lip, she looked away.

He wrapped his arm around her shoulders and hugged her to him. Comforting her he looked around again to see if there was anything that might not be normal. Shaking herself, she said, "Don't mind me. I'm sure it's nothing. It just felt like someone was watching me. I'm sure with Rob and Jemma's display a few moments ago we have more than one pair of eyes on us." She squeezed his hand and turned toward the apartment.

*   *   *   *   *   *   *   *

Back inside the apartment Ericka pushed aside the moment to concentrate on Jemma's kids. She loved being the boys' and Erin's Auntie. Jemma had gotten Erin out of her car seat and was changing her so Ericka gave her full attention to the boys, specifically Tom, who told her all about the flight. She was laughing and nodding at all the right parts of his story but Ericka was still shaky. She had felt every hair on her neck raise again just like last night at graduation. She didn't understand what was happening but added to her flashback dreams something was definitely happening. She just hoped that it would stay away while everyone was here. She looked up and saw Steven watching her. She tried to give him a reassuring smile but she could tell he wasn't buying it. She was going to have to have a chat with him. She knew it had been coming but these feelings seem to be forcing her hand.

Jemma came out of the room and Ericka jumped up and ran at her, "Give me, give me." She said taking Erin from Jemma's hands. Jemma laughed and settled in next to Rob. Tom came and sat next to her. Those two were very seldom apart. Tom had really taken to Jemma and considered her his momma.

Ericka sat down next to Luke and Steven. Playing with Erin on her lap. She was such a yummy baby. Ericka couldn't get enough of her. She had noticed how her biological clock had been ticking louder lately. She wished for the type of relationship Jemma and Rob had, but was afraid. She looked over at Steven and he smiled at her, making her stomach flip. There was definitely something there, but should she pursue it or step back? That was the question. She needed to tell him her whole story though. He may not want anything to do with her after learning what has happened and sadly what is still happening, although to be fair it had been a few years since New York.

Erin was getting fussy and Jemma smiled, "Looks like someone is hungry."

Luke said she wasn't the only one. They all laughed. Jemma took Erin into the bedroom to feed her and Ericka got up and went to the kitchen. Steven followed. "Are you sure you're ok Ericka?"

She went and grabbed the take-out menus from the side of the fridge. Taking them to the counter she spread them all out before replying, "I'm fine really. But I think the four of us need to have a little late-night chat. There is something about my past that you and Rob should know. Jemma already knows everything."

Pushing off from the counter Steven came over to her, "Are you in some kind of trouble?"

"Not that I know of but we will talk about everything later. I promise." She pointed to the menus, "Now help me choose what we will have for dinner."

Enlisting the boys' help, they decided on Chinese for dinner. That ordered and Erin fed, they decided to play some games before dinner arrived. It was a wonderful evening and just the distraction that Ericka really needed. She knew she would be telling her story later but tried to push those thoughts aside. Around 11 o'clock, Rob and Jemma put the boys to bed. They had set up an air mattress in their room so all three of them were able to share the room. While she waited, she cleaned up after their dinner and game of spoons. She needed to keep herself busy or she might lose her courage to delve into her past.

Grabbing a bottle of wine and 4 glasses she headed back to living room and waited for Rob and Jemma. She had just sat down when they came out. Erin was asleep in her porta crib in Rob and Jemma's room. Jemma went to check on her while Rob came and got a glass of wine. "Jemma said you wanted to talk to us. Is everything ok?" He asked while twirling the wine in his glass.

Ericka nodded and smiled. Glancing down the hall she saw Jemma emerge from her room. "Jemma knows what I'm about tell you both but it's time you both know the story too." She turned to Jemma who took her hand in hers and squeezed. Rob noticed the gesture and sat forward. Steven took Ericka's other hand and squeezed it as well.

She stood. "I'm not exactly sure where to start actually. But I know you know about my "special" talent. Just know as I tell you my story that my talent really doesn't help me very often." She laughed to herself. She began pacing the living room and began again. "I have been having reoccurring dreams the past couple of weeks. They are always the same one and last night at graduation and today in the parking lot my neck tingled. Now I know that sounds funny but with my talent you learn to look for these signs that something is off, whether good or bad. Now adding that tingle to the nature of my dreams tells me that something is wrong, and it more than likely has to do with Chad."

Jemma stood up. "Do you think he has found you again?"

Shrugging Ericka quietly said, "I don't know what it means."

Rob stood as well and took Ericka's hands in his. "Are you in danger?"

This made Steven jump up. "Danger? Will someone please explain to me what is going on? What do you mean found you again?"

Ericka pulled her hands from Rob and went to Steven. "I need to tell you both my story."

Rob took Jemma's hand and led her back to the couch. "Take your time Ericka. We aren't going anywhere."

Taking a deep cleansing breath, she started. "I guess the best place to start is at the beginning. My birth name is not Ericka Taylor, it was Anne Chandler, but everyone called me Annie. My parents died in a car crash when I was young. I went to live with my aunt and uncle after the crash. I grew up in a small town in the Midwest. I met Chad right out of high school. We dated for six months before we got married. Then I became Annie Hadley. At first life as a young married couple was great." Looking at Rob and Jemma, she smiled, "You two know all about that. That time where you can't keep your hands off each other." Jemma blushed and leaned into Rob's arm while he laughed.

It was the perfect tension breaker. Everyone started to slowly relax. "Well after a year, Chad started changing. I wasn't sure what was going on. It was like a light switch had been switched off and the man I fell in love with was gone. I found out later that he had lost his job and had started using

45

drugs. He changed quickly and not for the better. The first time he hit me I thought he had been playing around and took things too far. But it kept happening and pretty soon he couldn't get aroused unless he was beating me while having sex. I tried to stop him but it seemed to enrage him even more and turned him on to the extreme. So eventually I just stopped fighting back." She stood now and started pacing.

"My neighbor, who was a sweet older lady, was very worried about the fights and the bruises. She helped me find a support group that was anonymous so I could start to get out of the situation. I moved out and filed a restraining order," Shaking her head, "Like that would stop him. Anyway, I had found a group that would help me with finding a job and an attorney to help me file for a divorce. By this time, he was livid and started threatening me in front of people. The group helped me to move since he found the place I had originally moved into. But any place that there was an Anne Chandler or Hadley he found me pretty fast. He refused to sign the divorce papers so I filed and had him served with the papers. Did you know you could file for divorce without your spouses' consent? I had no idea until this happened. But I'm very grateful because it allowed me to move forward. Although every time I moved, he would find me. My friend from our support group suggested talking to an attorney about changing my name. It would be harder to find me if he didn't know my name. So, that is what I did. I changed my name. And it worked. I moved to New York and thought I'd get lost in the big city. A new name, a new town and a new life. Well, it worked for the longest time. But he found me," sitting down next to Steven she whispered, "He always finds me."

"I was waiting for my take-out order to arrive, so when the knock on my door came, I didn't even question it. I had gotten lazy and it was the opening he needed. He barged into my apartment, hit my lip splitting it open and eventually knocking me unconscious. But I managed eventually to use a glass vase to smash it against his head. He went down hard and I grabbed my go bag and left. I initiated my emergency plan, called my contact, checked my supplies and eventually made it to Grand Central Station. I met an amazing couple Mary and George Howard. Mary had been in a previous relationship like mine and saw the signs from the beginning. They were headed home to Atlanta and took me with them. I don't know if I would have made it to Los Angeles if I hadn't met them. George was a big guy and was alert for any disturbance, which allowed me to take a few deep breaths and think. I stayed with them in Atlanta for a while before making my journey here."

She stood again and poured herself a glass of wine. "My friend Grace told me that Chad had been arrested but fled custody at the hospital. There is still an outstanding warrant out for his arrest but he has evaded being arrested. When I first came to LA, I was introduced to my support group here and made similar emergency plans. I moved around a lot the first year here in town. But I had been able to start school. I needed to get a degree somehow in order to find a job. Luckily that same school is where I met Jemma. Having lived with Chad, I noticed the signs of abuse and because Mary and George had reached out a helping hand to me, I felt the need to do the same. And the rest is history." She drank deeply. "It has been almost two years since I have heard anything about Chad. But he is still out there. Legally we are no longer married but he refuses to acknowledge the divorce or the restraining order. In his crazy mind we are still married and I am just a wife being difficult."

Standing she went to the closet and grabbed her go back and dumped it out. There on the floor was a change of clothes, a wig, a cell phone, money and sunglasses. She picked up the sunglasses, "Mary gave me these when she saw me in the bathroom in New York. My lip was cut open and my eye was already black. She gave the sunglasses to me to cover my eye. They have been in my go bag ever since." Looking up she locked gazes with Steven.

"I have been having reoccurring dreams about that night in New York and how I got away. Last night after graduation, the hairs on the back of neck stood up as we were getting into the car. I looked around but only saw graduates and their loved ones. But I could have sworn someone was watching us. Then today while we were heading back up to the apartment after Rob arrived, I had the same feeling." Putting her head in her hands she shook her head. "I just don't know what it means. When I see things like Jemma being pregnant with Erin, it is super clear. I knew without a doubt. But when it comes to me and seeing things, it's never clear. But I have to think this has something to do with Chad. Maybe he is back, maybe he is looking for me again. I should have changed my name when I moved to LA but I was just tired. Tired of running and never having a family. So, when Jemma moved in, she became my family."

Jemma reached out and took her hands. "And I am so glad you are my family! We will figure this out. No more running. I can't lose you Ericka."

Steven placed his hand on her knee, "You aren't alone this time. If this has something to do with Chad, we will face it together." Entwining their fingers, he squeezed her hand.

Rob being the ever practical of the group asked, "Do you have any pictures of him by chance? I'd love to have my guy look into him if you don't mind. We have more resources now than you did back then. You are family Ericka and we take care of our family."

Closing her eyes, Ericka let the tears flow. She couldn't remember the last time she had this kind of support. She had always done things on her own. It was so nice having them around her. Letting go of her hand Steven put his arm around her and pulled her to his chest, which made the tears flow faster. She felt so safe in Steven's arms. She knew that whatever was between them was going to be life changing. For the good or bad she wasn't quite sure yet. She was already so confused with the situation with Chad, adding Steven into the mix may not be the best thing, but she wasn't going to turn down his support. She was so lonely and tired of being strong. Pulling back, she looked into Steven's eyes and saw her own emotions of confusion, sadness, anger and loneliness all reflected back at her.

*   *   *   *   *   *   *   *

They spent the next thirty minutes writing down all the details. What he looked like, date of birth, place of birth, last known address and job. Rob promised he would contact his guy in the morning and have him get started researching him. Rob said, "Another thing Ericka. I don't think you should go anywhere alone for the time being. You never know what could happen. It is lucky that we are all leaving day after tomorrow."

Steven took her hand and said, "She will not be by herself. I will keep an eye on her until we find him."

Rob grinned at Steven and said, "I thought that might be the case." Jemma looked at Rob and then Steven.

"What am I missing?" She asked Rob.

Kissing her hand, Rob said, "Don't worry. It's nothing."

Jemma looked skeptical but let it go for now. Steven looked at Ericka. She was still snuggled up to his chest and to be perfectly honest, he didn't want to let her go. He felt super protective of her after hearing her story and how brave she was. She had been through so much and all on her own. That changes today. He didn't know what would come from this flirtation but one thing was for sure. He would not let anything happen to Ericka again.

*   *   *   *   *   *   *   *

Sitting in the truck he watched as the lights finally went off in Annie's apartment. Seeing all those kids get out of her car and head inside had almost caused him to pick up and head out of town. But then he had seen Annie stop and look around with that scared look in her eyes. He knew she felt his presence. But then that guy pulled her into his arms. It was almost enough to make him jump out of the truck. Only the presence of the others caused him to think about what he was going to do. The arrival of so many other people in just the past two days felt like the universe was ganging up on him. Had he known where that guy had gone this morning, he would have just burst into her apartment while he was gone, but no he had to wait it out. Now there were so many other people here. The plans he had made were destroyed. He needed to regroup and figure out when she would be alone again.

He settled in for the night. Another night in the truck. He knew it was just a matter of time before he had his hands on Annie again. She has caused so much trouble these past years. He was really going to enjoy taking his revenge on her. And with that thought he drifted to sleep dreaming of Annie and their future.

Chapter 3

The next morning after a few cups of coffee to wake them up, it was time to take the kids and go explore the city. They decided to go on a bus tour to see the sites. Spending the day in the city was great. It was the distraction they needed to get through the day. Not once, did Ericka's neck tingle. Both Rob and Steven had made her swear she would alert them if she felt or saw anything unusual. Steven never once left her side and several times even held her hand. It was a nice day with some of her favorite people.

They decided to grab pizza after the long day and just relax that evening. Tomorrow they would all fly out to Oregon to the Morgan reunion. Paige had already called and complained that no one told her they were partying in LA. Laughing they took it all in stride. Cleaning up after the movie and while Rob and Jemma put the kids to bed, Ericka decided to run the trash out to the dumpster really quick.

As she made it to the dumpster her neck started tingling again. But as she looked around, she heard Steven calling to her from the stairs and ran down to help her. "You should have let me do this, Ericka."

Laughing she said, "It's just trash Steven. I'm sure I can handle a trash run."

Taking her face in his hands he looked into her eyes, "Yes but we don't want to take any chances with you. I would never forgive myself." Place a gentle kiss to her lips, she gasped. Dropping his hands he said, "I am sorry I should not have done that. I just couldn't help it."

Taking his face in her hands she kissed him. Not the gentle kiss like his, but a fierce and passionate kiss. Shocked at first Steven didn't respond until she started to pull away. He grabbed her and kissed her back. This time he was not so gentle. Wrapping her arms around his neck she tried to pull him closer. Ericka could not get close enough to him. The sound of someone clearing their throat penetrated the haze that enveloped them. They both turned toward the building to see Rob on the porch smiling. Placing her forehead on Steven's chest she groaned. Steven was rubbing her arms up and down and started chuckling. "Well, that was the best trash run I've ever been on."

Ericka laughed so hard she couldn't breathe. Wrapping her arms around one of Steven's, they started walking back to the apartment. "Then you have been visiting the wrong dumpsters sir."

Laughing, Steven kissed her forehead. "So true my dear. This dumpster is far superior to any I've visited in the past."

They were almost to the door when Ericka felt the eyes on her again. Whispering to Steven she said, "Someone is watching us, Steven."

They stopped and looked around. Nothing seemed amiss but he too felt the gaze of someone. "Ok let's get you into the apartment." Cupping her cheek, he said, "Don't worry though, Rob and I are not going to let anything happen to you."

She turned and kissed his palm. "Thank you, Steven." She locked gazes with him and raised up and kissed him lightly on the lips.

"What was that for?" Steven asked.

"For you of course but also for whoever is watching. If it is Chad, I want to make it perfectly clear I am not his." She answered.

"What does that make us then?" he asked grinning at Ericka.

"That is yet to be determined my good sir." She said saucily as she walked up the remaining steps. She wasn't sure but she thought she heard him say 'minx', as she walked off.

*   *   *   *   *   *   *   *

The sound of her apartment door shutting woke him up. Today had been one of the longest days of the whole trip. He had watched as the entire group walked and got on a bus. There was no way he would be able to keep up with them in that thing. He decided to wait them out, sitting in the parking lot. He must have fallen asleep though. He was still a bit disoriented when he saw Annie walking down the stairs with the trash; alone. He quietly got out of the truck. He had to make his way to the dumpster without being seen, which meant he had to come from the other side of the enclosure.

Making his way through the cars he chuckled to himself. How lucky was it that she was out here by herself? He could grab her and get away without anyone knowing. He just had to be quick and quiet. He came around the corner only to see that other guy making his way to the dumpster, talking to Annie. Damnit! He couldn't snatch her now. But maybe he could knock the guy out and grab her before anyone noticed. He was just about to come around the corner when he saw Annie grab the guy and kiss him. And not just some peck it was a devouring kiss. He froze. Standing there watching his wife in a passionate embrace wiped all thought from his mind. He just saw red. He was about to charge in when he heard the other guy clear his throat. He backed up quietly watching the exchange. When Annie stopped on the stairs and looked around, he almost smiled. Serves her right for kissing another man. When the guy looked around, he wished he would see him. Just so he would know just how much he hated him. But that would ruin everything so he melted into the dark shadows of the building and watched as they had yet another kiss. He really needed to figure out when they were leaving so he could exact his revenge.

*   *   *   *   *   *   *   *

Once inside the apartment they locked all locks, shut the windows and told Rob what they believe to be going on outside. Steven knew he would get little sleep tonight but it was fortunate that he was sleeping in the living room. He could keep an eye on things without disrupting the rest of the family. He couldn't wait to get everyone to Mom and Dad's place so they all could breathe a little easier and come up with some type of plan to help Ericka get through this. They really needed to get this guy so she had a chance to start her life over. Whether or not he would be in that life he was still unsure about, but man that kiss, whew. He was getting hard just thinking about it. The fact that she instigated the passionate kiss surprised, but delighted, him. Now if they could just explore where this was going without any crazy ex-husbands that would be fantastic.

Inside they found Rob on the phone. "Dad we just need a little extra protection. Can you please send a guy to the Morgan's to meet us tomorrow? We are fine but I would feel better with an extra pair of eyes." There was a pause and they could hear mumbling from the phone. "No, you do not need to fly out too."

Jemma walked to Rob and placed a hand on his arm. "Mom said she had invited your dad and grandpa, Rob. If he wants to come, he would be welcome. But only if it does not interfere with his work or plans."

Nodding, Rob addressed his dad. "Did you hear Jemma dad? Great. Ok we will see you day after tomorrow then."

Ericka sat on the couch shaking her head, "I have caused so much trouble. Maybe I should just stay here so I don't put any of you in Chad's cross hairs."

Steven sat next to her and took her hand in his. "If he is the one you are sensing, he has already seen all of us. He would come to us looking for you. It's safer if we all stay together."

Rob nodded. "He is right Ericka. Besides you are family. I would never leave you to deal with this on your own. I would never forgive myself, let alone Jemma would never forgive me either, if something happened to you and we could have prevented it."

Steven wrapped his arm around Ericka, and she leaned into him. "I'm just not used to having this kind of support. It's hard to accept help even if I know what you are saying is true." Looking up into Steven's face then turning to Rob and Jemma. "Thank you. You don't know how much I appreciate all of this."

Standing Ericka and Steven joined Rob and Jemma. After a group hug Rob and Jemma went to bed. Ericka was still puttering around the living room cleaning up. Steven stopped her and took both her hands in his. "It's ok. I know you are nervous but please know we won't let anything happen to you."

He brushed the back of his knuckles along her cheek. Ericka closed her eyes and stepped closer. Steven brought his other hand to her hip. "Ericka, what are we doing?" He whispered.

She opened her eyes and shook her head, "I don't know, Steven. But I don't want to stop."

She brought her hand up to the back of Steven's head, pulling him down toward her. She covered his mouth with hers making Steven groan. Grabbing her hip with his free hand, he brought her even closer deepening the kiss. He traced her lip with his tongue encouraging her to open to him. She slid her tongue into his mouth, and started a mating dance with her tongue. Pulling Steven closer she pressed her body up against him. He was quickly losing his control. He reached around and grabbed her glorious bottom. Lifting her slightly and pulling her toward the evidence of his desire. She gasped in his mouth and he pulled back slightly to look into her eyes. "Make me to stop, Ericka! For God's sake make me stop." Kissing the underside of her jaw and making his way down her neck, she arched into him as he kissed her collarbone.

The sound of a door closing brought them back to where they were and who was there. Pressing one last kiss on her lips he placed his forehead to hers, he whispered, "Ericka". He took a step back not releasing her completely though.

Smiling up at Steven, Ericka placed her hand on his cheek and said, "You are a good man, Steven Morgan. I would like to see where this path leads us."

"Me too." He whispered, turning to kiss her palm. "Just hopefully not with a potential audience."

That made her laugh, which is what he had intended. Some of the tension left their bodies and they sat down on the couch. Neither one wanting the other to leave. With his arm around Ericka and her tucked up against his chest they talked until they both drifted to sleep on the couch both content in each other's arms.

Chapter 4

Steven was having a wonderful dream. He and Ericka were walking hand in hand along the beach. Talking and chatting like normal, except he couldn't keep his hands from touching her. She slipped her hands up inside his shirt to feel his chest and looked up into his face. He felt her push him and say his name. "Steven, wake up."

Waking with a start, he opened his eyes. He tried to turn to see who was pushing him and realized he must have slept in an awkward position since his neck was aching. But looking down he saw Ericka asleep on his chest with his arm wrapped around her.

A throat being cleared alerted him to someone else in the room. Turning he saw a grinning Rob and frowning Jemma. "What do you think you are doing Steven?" Jemma asked.

"I was sleeping before I was rudely interrupted. Although my neck thanks you." He retorted.

Huffing, Jemma crossed her arms in front of her chest. "That's not what I meant and you know it."

"It's not his fault Jemma." Ericka said as she sat up. "We were up talking into the night and we both fell asleep."

Humph. "Well, the boys are up and we need to get started for our trip today.

Steven and Ericka stood and stretched out their sore muscles. Grinning at Rob, he excused himself to use the restroom. He needed to gather his thoughts and try and figure out what he is doing.

The morning flew by as everyone prepared to leave. They loaded up the two taxis with their luggage and headed to the airport. Once safely on the plane Ericka was able to take a deep cleansing breath. Even if Chad was in LA stalking her, she was gone now and he wouldn't know where she had gone or when she would return.

*   *   *   *   *   *   *   *

One good thing about having so many people at Annie's apartment was they were loud. Luckily, he was able to overhear parts of a conversation about the airport. He just needed to find out where they were headed and if it was some place he could follow. Later that morning as the two oldest kids took the trash to the dumpster, he was able to over hear them talking about heading to Oregon and seeing grandma and grandpa Morgan. "Just remember Luke, Portland Airport is big so we will need to stay together and keep an eye on Tom." The tall child said. Nodding the younger one said, "Do you think we will be able to ride the four-wheelers this time Charlie?" But Chad didn't hear the response as they were almost to the apartment by then. They were headed to Portland. That is a long drive but totally doable. Getting in his truck he decided not to wait and to get driving now. He would have to look up the address when he got closer. It was going to be a long drive but if he could grab her there it would cut time off the trip home.

*　　*　　*　　*　　*　　*　　*　　*

Traveling with such a large group can be fun but also chaotic. Luckily the adults, and Charlie counted himself in that category now, out-numbered the kids. She was glad that she was not seated on the flight near any of the family to be honest. She needed that time to clear her mind and refocus. The past few days' activities had happened so suddenly, which she was so glad they were there, but it was a lot to take in, in such a short period of time. First, Steven showing up on her doorstep, next came Jemma, then graduation and then Rob and kids, all within 48 hours had arrived at her home. Not to mention her feelings for Steven evolving and the strange sensations that she was being watched. It was a lot to try and sift through. The time on the plane was a great time to just breathe and clear her thoughts.

Landing in Portland, they were greeted by Paige and Trevor Morgan. "I'm so glad you all were able to come. We are going to have a great visit." Paige said.

Jemma said, "About that mom, we have something we need to talk about when we get home." She looked at Ericka and lowering her voice said, "It's about Chad."

Paige turned to Ericka and enfolded her in her arms, whispering, "Are you ok sweetheart?"

She was trying to hold back the tears. With her throat tight she replied, "I'm ok. We can talk more when we get to your place though."

After heading to baggage claim they loaded up the vehicles and headed to the Morgan's home. Grant and Cindy were already at the house.

Ericka had been a little nervous about this trip. She had spent lots of time with Jemma's family, but was worried about Chad. She was also a little nervous about Steven. They had that moment by the dumpster, which should go down the in the 'worst ever' location to seduce someone book. The kiss in the kitchen though, was some kiss. They did need to talk about what happened. This was a different path than their relationship had been on before. They were great friends and Ericka really cared about Steven and his friendship. He was so easy to talk to and never judgmental. She didn't want to lose that portion of their relationship but was curious and excited to see if this new path would be even better.

Steven was gorgeous with his dark brown hair and green eyes. He was pretty tall, well over six feet. He was not stocky but he was muscular. He was strong; she had felt that when he had pulled her into his arms and hard chest. She closed her eyes and thought about that kiss and warmth seemed to fill her veins and travel through her body all converging between her thighs. She had never reacted this way to anyone before. Since Chad she had the occasional relationship or fling but this was something else. Something she couldn't quite put her finger on. Her concern now though was being here with him and his entire family while exploring where this might lead.

Now as they all made their way to the Morgan's home; she was reminded of just how much she loved this family. Crammed in the vehicles, everyone was excited and full of energy. Luckily it wasn't too far to the house. Ericka got to ride next to Charlie in the van with Tom and Luke in front of them and Steven up front with Trevor. Rob, Jemma and Erin all rode with Paige. Pulling up to the house, Grant and Cindy came out and greeted everyone and helped with bags and kids. The boys piled out of the van while Steven waited and reached in to help her scoot across the bench seat to get out. Standing up, she smiled and locked gazes with Steven while he rubbed his thumb on the back of her hand. Tingles shot up her arm and her breath caught.

Luke came running over to Steven and said, "We get to sleep in a tent Uncle Steven. This is my first-time camping." With the moment gone, Steven gave Ericka's hand a squeeze and let go. Turning to Luke he said, "You are going to have a lot of fun. The great thing is you are camping right next to the house so you will be close to the kitchen. I know you are always hungry." He wrapped his arm around his shoulder and squeezed him. "Did you get all your things?" he asked while walking to the back of the van.

*   *   *   *   *   *   *   *

Steven needed to clear his mind. Ericka had been filling his thoughts since their kisses and had there been no one here now, he would have repeated those kisses. It was a good thing Luke interrupted when he did or he may have done it anyway. Grabbing his and Ericka's bags he started toward her. She reached out to take her bag and he said, "I have it. I'm not sure where Mom put you though. I'm assuming in the spare room, which is actually her crafting room now."

She smiled at him. "Thank you. I am pretty easy to please, all I need is a bed and I'm good to go." As soon as the words left her mouth, Steven knew she wished she could recall them. She staggered a couple steps and then corrected herself. She would not look at Steven. He knew her face was bright red and Steven chuckled. She must have heard him as her shoulders went rigid. She knew Steven had caught the inuendo. Climbing the stairs, Jemma came out and wrapped her arm around Ericka's and showed her where she was staying. Steven followed with her bag. Placing the bag on the floor just inside the door, he turned and looked at Ericka, he smiled at her and left to go to his room.

*   *   *   *   *   *   *   *

Jemma was excited to have Ericka with the family and was looking forward to showing her where she grew up. She also caught that look between her and Steven. Rob told her about him catching them kissing at the dumpster. She really needed to talk to Steven about that. A dumpster was no place to kiss someone. She was excited though to see they had finally taken the next step. She had been watching their friendship blossom and had always hoped they would realize just how perfect they were for each other. This trip home would be a great chance to throw them together often.

"Feel up for a tour? I can show you around and where everything is and where everyone is staying." Jemma asked.

"I'd love a tour." Ericka replied.

Jemma took her from the craft room back to the front door. "Ok I want to start outside. The porch is one of my favorite places. The porch wraps around the entire house with benches or swings placed all around. The patio has the grill. Off to the right there is the basketball court. Off to the left is the fire pit. And just down that path straight ahead, is the river. The boys will be setting up the tent there on the lawn next to the fire pit."

They went back inside and Jemma showed Ericka the family room, dining room, and kitchen. They were starting up the stairs to the family rooms, when Steven was coming down. The stairs were a bit snug which allowed Steven and Ericka to brush up against each other. Tingles shot through her body. Looking over her shoulder, Ericka watched as Steven continued walking down the stairs with his hands clenched in fists. He must have felt that too. Jemma cleared her throat and Ericka turned her attention back to the tour. Jemma showed her the rest of the house, but Ericka's thoughts were downstairs with Steven. She wondered if he too had felt those tingles when they met on the stairs or if she was over thinking this.

With the tour complete they joined everyone in the family room. The Morgan family was a fun and loving family. Everyone was happy and just enjoying visiting with each other. Ericka had found a rocking chair and was enjoying the banter between the adult siblings. Being an only child, she never experienced anything like this. Her childhood had been a bit lonely.

Pretty soon it was time for dinner. Everyone filed outside to the patio and with the tables full of food they feasted while chatting, laughing and truly enjoying themselves. It was beautiful here. There were so many shades of green in the mountains and against that bright blue sky, it was just breathtaking. The Morgan's lived on a what appeared to be a few acres. Everyone was relaxing at the table, no one really wanting the evening to end. But as Tom's head drooped again, they knew it was time for bed.

The men had set the tent up while Ericka was on the tour so the boys all went back inside the house to change and get ready. Jemma came back out after helping the boys and laughing she turned to Rob and said, "I have a feeling we might have an extra person in our bed sometime tonight."

"I thought as much but he wants to be like his big brothers." Rob said while laughing.

*   *   *   *   *   *   *   *

Ericka stood to help clear the table. She was piling plates on top of each other when Steven walked up next her reaching for the cups. His hand was still tingling from the brush against Ericka on the stairs. So, when he went to go around her, he made sure to accidentally brush up against her again. When she stood upright, he turned and smiled at her. She was blushing and her breath had caught in her throat. He smiled even bigger realizing that she was not unaffected by him. When he looked back at her, her eyes smoldered with fire. His breath caught and he missed a step. Stumbling, he righted himself, he turned back to see she had moved on to gather more plates. He turned and headed into the house almost running over Rob who was grinning and looking back and forth between him and Ericka. *'Oh great'* he thought to himself. It was bad enough that Rob had caught them at the dumpster kissing. Now he was catching him make a fool of himself.

In the kitchen, he put the glasses on the counter to be loaded into the dishwasher. Ericka came in carrying a stack of dishes, almost as tall as her. Laughing he took some of her stack. "Are you trying to make me look bad?" he asked.

71

"Nah I'm just used to bussing tables. I have been a server at many restaurants through the years. Time is money, so you learn to bus your tables quickly." She responded.

Grabbing a towel, she turned and walked back outside to get another load. Steven couldn't resist the temptation and as she walked to the door, he snapped his towel at her bottom. Gasping she turned and saw Steven with his towel grinning from ear to ear. Ericka raised her eyebrow and smirked at him saying, "Really? I'm not sure you could handle a towel fight. I am somewhat of a pro."

Laughing he winked at her. "Try me."

"Well, anyone can snap a towel at a person, that's a fairly large target." She stated.

"Wait are you saying you are large? 'Cuz, you don't look large to me." He retorted, while looking up and down her body. His eyes took in all her loveliness.

Ericka blushed and smacked his shoulder playfully saying, "No. I meant large in comparison to say a soda can. I challenge you Steven Morgan to a duel. Weapon of choice is a dish towel and instead of people we will use soda cans as targets. Most knocked off the fence wins and the loser must fulfill a request of the winner." Arms now folding across her chest she had gotten Rob and Grant's attention.

Stepping closer to Ericka, Steve reached out his hand and said, "Challenge Accepted who is your second? Mine will be Rob."

Stepping closer to Steven, she looked over to Grant who smiled and nodded at her. Taking Steven's hand, she shook it and answered, "My second will be Grant. We will commence the duel after breakfast. I know how growing boys need their food."

Steven used his hand still clenched with Ericka's to pull her even closer and whispered for her ears only, "I'm going to enjoy this and the request I will give you."

Laughing he let Ericka go and she turned to walk back outside but stopped at the door. Turning she said, "I wouldn't bet on it." Then walked outside.

Steven turned to look at Grant and Rob. Both were trying to hold in their laughter, but failing miserably. "Go ahead, get it out of your system." He groaned.

"Which part, the growing boy comment or the fact you are having a duel with dish towels?" Grant said.

Rob said, "Oh, I think both are deserving of a good laugh. I knew I stumbled onto something at Ericka's." He said as he came over and smacked his shoulder.

"I'm not even sure what you stumbled on, but I am more than a little curious to find out more." Steven smiled and went into the family room leaving both Grant and Rob laughing in his wake.

*   *   *   *   *   *   *   *

What had Ericka just done? She just challenged Steven to a duel. And not just any duel, but one with a dish towel. She needed to enlist some help. Going to the table she walked over to Jemma and started gathering dishes. "I need your help Jemma. I just challenged Steven to a dish towel duel tomorrow."

Jemma stopped and looked up. "You did what?"

"I know, ridiculous right? But he snapped me with a dish towel so I challenged him. I'm going to need to set up targets with empty cans or bottles." She paused while still grabbing dirty dishes. "I'm not sure how to plan the challenge. I guess the one who knocks their targets down first wins. What do you think?" She turned back to Jemma.

Jemma was just standing there with her jaw hanging open. "Ok let me get this straight. You challenged Steven to a duel using towels because he snapped you with one?" She asked.

Ericka nodded and Jemma burst into laughter. "Only you would come up with a dish towel duel. Whatever that is." Laughing harder she tried to catch her breath. "I am so glad you are here Ericka. And yes, I will help you."

While finishing outside they came up with the challenge and figured out what the targets would be. Cindy and Paige both came out when they heard from Rob and Grant what had happened. They wanted to help with this duel. Pretty soon they were all sitting at the table planning out the day. Ericka was laughing so hard at some of the stories that Paige told on Grant and Steven. Ericka turned to the look back at the house and saw Steven standing in the doorway leaning against the door watching the women. He smiled at her and winked. She smiled back then turned back to Jemma who was correcting Paige on an incident.

Time flew by. They would need to gather everything for the duel in the morning. The details all planned out, they headed to bed. Ericka's room was the only room on the ground floor. She was just coming out of the bathroom after brushing her hair and teeth when she ran into Steven who was waiting for her in the hallway. "I just wanted to check on you to make sure you had everything you needed and to make sure you weren't mad about earlier. I really was just playing around." He said as he stepped closer.

She smiled at him and placed her hand on his chest. "I'm fine really. I was just having a bit of fun with you. And I think I have everything I need."

Stepping closer he looked down at her lips and whispered, "Are you sure you have everything you want?"

She stepped closer to him, so their bodies were almost touching. Quickly licking her lips, she smiled at him, "That's not what you asked. You asked if I had what I needed. Now having what I want is different." She whispered.

His hands went to her hips and he looked down at her lips again. She looked into his eyes and wound her arm around his neck pulling him closer and lifted onto her tip toes. Covering his mouth with hers, she kissed him. Growling he wound his arms around her waist and pulled her up against him, causing her to gasp. Taking advantage, he slipped his tongue into her mouth and kissed her deeply. Moving his hand to the back of her head he held her in place while he mapped the inside of her mouth with his tongue. She pulled him closer and moaned as his other hand slid up from her waist to her breast. She arched into him and pretty soon they were both panting.

Pulling back Steven said, "I am not sorry I started this, but I need to finish it before someone comes down."

Resting his forehead against hers, she whispered his name, "Steven," cupping his cheek she said, "Are you ready for our duel? We have it all planned out."

He smiled and kissed her temple, "I have my request all ready to go." His voice was lower and bit more husky than normal.

"I wouldn't be too cocky now. You haven't seen my towel snapping skills. I could be a ringer and you'd have to obey my request." She retorted.

"Oh, I'm totally ready to obey any request you have my dear. I just know that I won't have too." He laughed.

"Oh really?! We will just see about that Mr. Morgan." She playfully swatted his shoulder.

Leaning in he captured her mouth again, causing her to moan and tilt her hips against him. Feeling how much he was wanting her. Groaning he pulled back again. "Ok I have to stop or I may not be able too."

Playfully pushing him away. She smiled at him went to her door stopping before entering to say good night. Walking into her room she closed the door and leaned against it trying to catch her breath. Oh, my goodness, she was all hot and bothered. Getting into bed, she realized just how tired she was and drifted to sleep thinking about Steven with a smile on her face.

Chapter 5

Morning came bright and early. Jemma had been correct about Tom. He had snuck into Jemma's room sometime in the night and climbed into their bed. Everyone was slowly waking up, so Jemma told the boys about the dish towel duel, that would be happening that morning, to keep them busy. After everyone had their breakfast and coffee, they started gathering what they needed for the duel. Trevor went and got two saw horses and set them up off the patio. Jemma and Paige gathered the empty cans and lined them up along the top of the saw horses. Cindy handed Steven and Ericka, along with Rob and Grant, dish towels. Ericka questioned the logic of giving Rob and Grant towels as they started chasing first their wives and then the boys with their towels. Laughing Jemma and Cindy confiscated Rob and Grant's towels for the betterment of the entire family.

After putting Erin down for a nap, Jemma ran out with the child monitor in hand saying, "Let's get started while Erin is sleeping. Ericka and Grant, you are on this side." She pointed to the left. "Steven and Rob, you are on the other side. Now instead of pacing you both meet in the middle and shake hands." Rob coughed at Jemma who said, "Oh yes, I almost forgot," she said rolling her eyes at Rob, she turned to Ericka and Steven. "Trash talking is allowed, even encouraged. Should you need assistance in that department your seconds have informed me they are more than ready."

Ericka and Steven walked to the middle and faced each other. All that was going through Steven's mind was the kiss from last night and how much he wanted a repeat of that right then. He looked down at her lips quickly and then back up to her eyes. Clearing his throat, he noticed Ericka's cheeks were pink. So, he wasn't the only one thinking about that kiss. He smiled at her and she returned that smile with a mischievous twinkle in her eyes. She quickly licked her lips, causing him to loo at her lips again, and then she smiled causing him to groan inwardly. She knew exactly what he was thinking. He was going to enjoy payback that is for sure. They reached out their hands to shake and Steven grabbed hers with both of his hands and rubbed his thumb back and forth on her palm. Bringing her hand up to his lips he kissed the back of her hand while their gazes locked. He noticed her pink cheeks darkened and her breathing became irregular. Good. She needed a bit of her own medicine.

A throat clearing behind him had him breaking eye contact with Ericka. "Steven, did you hear a word I just said? Let go of Ericka, she is going to need both hands." Jemma said as she stood there with hands on her hips. Rob and Grant were laughing. He turned and gave them a look that should have been stern but it just made them laugh even more. "Listen Steven, I'm explaining the rules."

Jemma went back to the saw horses and said, "There are five cans on each saw horse. You will be standing no closer than the line drawn in the grass. If you knock more than one can off at a time, all cans that fell will be returned to the saw horse. So, you will need to be precise in your aiming. You will alternate snaps and there will be three rounds. The one with the most cans knocked off will be the winner. At any time, you cannot finish any round your second will step in and finish that round." Turning to Steven, "Did you listen that time?" Steven smiled and nodded at Jemma. "Good. We will begin with Ericka since she is the one who challenged you to this duel. Please step up to the line and get ready."

Ericka stepped up and shook out her towel to get it in just the right position. Rolling her shoulders to release some tension, she turned to Jemma and nodded. She blew the whistle to start the round. Ericka aimed at the closest can to Steven's side. With just a tap of the end of the towel, the can fell to the ground. Luke was Ericka's score keeper and Tom, with the help of grandma Paige, was the score keeper for Steven. Luke held up the number one.

Then it was Steven's turn. He stepped up and shook out his towel like Ericka did. *What's good for the goose is good for the gander, right?* He aimed and knocked off one can. Tom jumped up with a number one. This went on back and forth until the end of the second round. Steven aimed and knocked two cans off. Groaning he watched as Cindy put both cans back up on the saw horse. This meant that Ericka was one ahead of him now. Finally, they were in the middle of round three when Ericka also knocked two cans down. Jemma quickly replaced them, bringing them both tied. Finishing the third round tied.

Turning to Paige, "Did we have a tie breaker?" Ericka asked.

Nodding Paige stood up. "The field will be reset and you each will be timed in your attempt to knock all 5 down, one at a time. The one with the quickest time will be the winner."

Jemma and Cindy reset the field and since Steven was the one challenged, he got to choose if he went first or last. He turned and looked at Ericka, "I will go last, I think. I want to watch how to do this correctly."

Trevor was the time keeper and said, "Are you ready Ericka?" She nodded at him and he said, "On your marks, get set, go."

And she was off, knocking one off at a time in a steady pace until the last one. She missed it. She aimed again, and missed it. Taking a deep breath, she relaxed and aimed and knocked it off. Getting her time of 10.32 seconds, she went and sat next to Luke on the bench.

Steven stood and walked to the line with his towel. He shook it out and got it ready. Steven knew he could beat her since she missed twice, but did he want to win? Dad asked if he was ready and he gave a slight nod. "On your marks, get set, go." He knocked the first one off, missed the second on purpose then tried again. He knocked off the second, third and fourth, missing the fifth and having to retry. Getting it on the next try, he wasn't sure if it was enough time for her to win or not. He walked over to his dad and looked at the stop watch 10.22 seconds. He looked up at his dad, then turned to Ericka and said "10.52 seconds. Great job Ericka." He walked over and shook her hand, while his dad quickly cleared and put away his stop watch. Steven knew he was going to get questioned later but by the smirk on his dad's face, Steven thought his dad had a pretty good idea what was going on.

All four of the ladies, Luke and Grant were cheering for Ericka. Rob walked over to Steven placing his hand on his shoulder and squeezed it. "Good try" he said. Steven just looked up at him and smiled. Rob looked at him with a raised eyebrow. "Oh. Well played my man." And he smacked him on the back and walked off to join Jemma.

All in all, it had been a super fun morning. The boys were now trying their hand at knocking off the cans with the dish towel with the encouragement of all the adults. They would ask Ericka questions, since she won after all, and she would get up and show them how she did it. Steven loved watching her interact with the boys and his family. It felt like a missing piece to their family had been found in Ericka. He wasn't quite ready to analyze that thought though.

Jemma came up beside and nudged him with her shoulder. "Thank you," she said. "I just talked to Rob." Turning to look at Steven she said, "You know how special she is right? She has a story of her own, like mine and Clint's, so please be careful with her. This is the first time I've ever seen her open up like this." She turned to look at Ericka.

Steven wrapped his arm around her shoulder and said, "Duly noted sister. Please know that I would never intentionally hurt her."

She slipped her arm around his waist and whispered, "I know. She has just been alone for so long I worry for her."

Nodding his head, he gave her a squeeze and kissed the top of her head. Rob watched from across the yard and raised an eyebrow. "Now if you could please tell your husband, I have not hurt you or anything before he comes over here, I'd greatly appreciate it." Jemma looked up and across the yard to Rob and laughed. Rob smiled and nodded. She let go of Steven and walked over and sat on Rob's lap.

The rest of the day flew by and before they knew it the sun had set. After dinner they talked about the next day and what ideas people had for adventures. Grant and Steven looked at each other and said at the same time, "Zip Line."

Charlie perked up at this and wanted to know more. Grant told Charlie all about the zip line on their property and how they would take the four wheelers to get there. He told them all about how grandpa Trevor had installed it when Grant was in high school and how much fun they used to have going up there with their friends. Rob told Luke and Tom would be allowed to go on the zipline too, with some adjustments to the zipline apparatus. They would take a picnic to the zip line and those who wanted to, could go on the line and the others could watch. They would have to wait until Rob's dad and his guard arrived before they could head there but it would be a super fun afternoon.

With that plan approved by all it was time for bed. Everyone trudged to the tent or upstairs for bed except Steven who stopped in the kitchen for a glass of water. He looked down the hall and saw Ericka's door closed with light coming from under the door and figured he missed his chance. He was walking past the family room when a hand reached out and grabbed his wrist. Pulling him into the room and pressing him up against the wall. "I know what you did Steven," she whispered into his ear sending a shiver through his entire body.

"Ericka, I don't know what you are talking about." He responded enjoying being pinned against the wall by Erica.

"I know you beat me this morning. But what I want to know is why you didn't shout from the roof tops that you beat me." She queried.

"It wasn't about beating you, Ericka. It was about having fun. We all had fun and that is what is the most important thing. I would do it again in a heartbeat." He started to move away from the wall.

She pushed him back against the wall. "Who said you could leave? I'm not done with you yet." Reaching up on tip toe she kissed his neck and whispered, "Thank you, Steven. But I still think I owe you a request."

She pulled back from him and let him up but as she stepped away from the wall, he reached out his arm and wrapped it around her to bring her back up against his chest. Whispering in her ear he said, "I will have to think long and hard about what request I want."

He nuzzled her neck and kissed it, nipping her ear lobe and pulling her closer to his chest. She pushed back with her bottom and rubbed against his erection. Growling he nipped and licked her neck where it met her shoulder making her gasp. He brought his other hand up and cupped her breast. Massaging it and her nipple. She moaned and laid her head back onto his shoulder, all while still moving her delicious bottom up against him. He needed to stop, he told himself. But as he was about to stop, she bent at her waist pushing even more against his erection. His hands moved to her hips and he mimicked what he really wanted to do to her, thrusting and rubbing himself against her bottom. He was going to embarrass himself if he didn't stop soon. Holding her to him he gently rubbed once more before reaching for her shoulders and turning her toward him, capturing her mouth with his with a kiss of desperation and longing. "You are going to be the death of me. You realize that don't you?" he said against her lips.

She smiled and replied, "Yes but what a way to go." And she gave him a quick kiss, said good night and left the room.

Inwardly groaning, he knew he wasn't getting much sleep tonight. He trudged upstairs to his room and threw himself onto his bed, staring at the ceiling. What was he doing? This connection between them was strong, almost overpowering. He was drawn to her but not just physically. His stomach flipped just hearing her voice. His heart sped up at every glance of her. He had never felt this way before which was significant itself. But the fire they had between them, whew. When they finally did come together, he wouldn't be surprised if they spontaneously combusted. She was bolder than the women he was used to dating. Maybe it was because they were friends first, and she felt she could be herself with him, which made him happy. He was loving this side of Ericka that most people didn't get to see. Laying there he thought about their friendship. It was definitely something he didn't want to lose. But man did he want her. He wanted her bad and had he not caught himself he would have taken her right there from behind in the family room. When she bent over in front of him, he'd almost spilled into his pants. She had felt so good pressed up against him. Rolling over he closed his eyes. He had to try and get some sleep, because tomorrow was another day full of fun and adventures. He had never enjoyed a family gathering more than this one and it all had to do with Ericka.

Chapter 6

Steven drug himself into the kitchen and straight to the coffee pot. He heard chuckling coming from the breakfast nook. Turning with his coffee he looked at his mom, who was smiling at him.

"Rough night son?" she asked.

Nodding, "Had trouble sleeping. I don't think I actually fell asleep until right before dawn." He yawned to emphasized his statement.

Laughing, she started to say something when the lady who had been plaguing his thoughts both while awake and while asleep walked into the kitchen bright and cheery. "Good morning. It's going to be a lovely day today. I was just coming for a refill."

Paige stood and refilled her cup and said, "I'll go see if anyone else needs more."

Ericka walked over and placed her hand on his shoulder. "Good morning, Steven."

Looking up into her face he smiled. "Good morning. You are awfully chipper this morning."

"I am excited about the zip line; I've never been on one before." She turned to leave but stopped at the door, "Oh and I had an amazingly inciteful dream last night. One that I feel may happen while on this trip." She then turned and headed back out to the patio where everyone who was up was having breakfast.

Intrigued Steven, followed her outside and filled his plate. *I wonder what that dream was about and how she knows it will happen this trip.* Looking around he noticed Rob and Dad were gone. "Where are Dad and Rob?" he asked.

"They went to pick up Mike and his guard from the airport." Jemma said.

"Oh, that's right I forgot they were coming in today." He replied.

"After they get here, we will all load up on the four-wheelers and head out to the zip line." Grant said. "Rob made me promise not to head out until then."

Later that morning with baskets of food and drinks ready to go, Steven said, "Why don't we make a run with a load of food and people? It's going to take us a few trips with only three, four-wheelers."

Nodding Grant agreed, "I was just thinking the same thing. How about we take Charlie, the food, and Ericka. We can leave them there to set up while we get more people. Cindy, why don't you take some of the food, I'll take Charlie and Ericka can ride with Steven."

Grinning at his brother, Steven said, "Sounds good let's do this."

With food strapped to the back of Cindy's four-wheeler, she followed behind Grant and Charlie with Steven and Ericka bringing up the rear. Before leaving Steven turned to Ericka and said, "Hold tight. It's a bumpy ride."

Ericka had no problem with doing that. Climbing up behind Steven she pressed her body into his back, wrapped her arms around him and laid her cheek on his back. Her heart was pounding in her ears. He felt so good. Then he placed a hand over hers and squeezed her hands. She snuggled closer to him and tried to calm her breathing.

Ok so maybe this wasn't a good idea. He thought to himself. He could feel her everywhere, with her breasts pushed up against his back and her arms wrapped around him, he was having a hard time concentrating. Then she snuggled closer and he could feel the heat of her core around his bottom and he almost pulled over and pulled her around to straddle him. He needed to focus. Charlie, Cindy and

Grant were all going to be at the zip line when they arrived and he couldn't get off the four-wheeler in his current condition without alerting every one of his desires.

*　*　*　*　*　*　*　*

Pulling up to the zip line area, Ericka looked around. There was what looked like a tree house in one of the largest trees she had ever seen. From that tree was a metal wire, or line stretching across an open pasture to another tree that was slightly smaller and shorter than the tree with the house. Under the treehouse there was a picnic table that Cindy was already filling with the stuff she brought with her. Pulling up next to Grant, Steven placed his hand on top of Ericka's hands. "As much as I don't want you to move, I have to go back and get more people." He said over his shoulder.

She tightened her hold on him instead of letting go and whispered, "Hurry back," into his ear then kissed his ear.

With a low growl only she could hear, he mumbled something that sounded like minx. Laughing she let go of him and with her hands on his hips for balance she squeezed him and swung her leg around and got off the four-wheeler. Just as she stood up, he grabbed her wrist and pulled her in for a quick kiss. Gasping she looked around but no one was watching them. "You are playing with fire my dear." He whispered then turned his four-wheeler back on. He and Grant left to head back to the house with Cindy.

Soon enough Grant, Steven and Rob all had brought more people. Luke and Tom rode with Steven while Jemma and Cindy both rode with their husbands. Paige had decided to stay at the house with Erin. Rob and Grant were going back for Mike and Trevor while Mike's guard stayed at the house with Paige and Erin.

Soon everyone was here and ready to get started. Trevor explained that Tom and Luke could go on the zipline but they had to wear helmets. Both boys were so excited. Trevor explained there was stairs leading up to the platform where there are handle bars they would place on the line. Each had rope tied to it with a seat in the middle so you could sit while holding on to the handle bars. Grant volunteered to go first to show everyone what to do. He climbed up to the platform with Trevor. Trevor helped him get up and Grant leaned forward off the platform and swung down and dropped into the seat while holding on to the handle bars. Then he zipped along the line down to the other tree. He would be the catcher they said. Basically, a catcher was someone who makes sure you get to the other platform and not fly off the end. There were two sets of handle bars but also there was a pulley system in place so the launcher,

Trevor, could pull the bars back from the bottom tree for the next two people.

Charlie and Jemma climbed up to meet Trevor. Jemma insisted that Charlie also wear a helmet. Groaning and rolling his eyes he put it on. Then followed Grant's example and zipped across the line. Jemma was next then Cindy brought Luke up. Trevor helped Luke get set up and with instructions not to let go of the handle he stepped off and zipped to Jemma's waiting arms. Cindy was next down the line.

Rob and Tom went up the stairs, leaving Steven, Mike and Ericka. They all watched as Tom put his helmet on and Rob helped him on the seat and lowered him over the edge. With his eyes closed Tom zipped down to Jemma and his brothers. Once caught by Jemma, the group collectively took a breath, that everyone had been holding. Tom was super excited but he was also mad because he had closed his eyes. He wanted to do it again so this time he could see.

Mike deferred to Ericka and Steven as he wasn't zipping today. Ericka and Steven climbed the stairs to the top. Ericka was first. She took the handle bars and started to swing out over the edge. She made it about half way when the seat came undone and the handle bars got stuck and stopped moving. Panicking she kicked and couldn't move the bars, but was just hanging there. Turning to look at the platform to find Steven already getting ready to come help. They locked eyes and he said, "I'm coming. Just hang on." She nodded at him and waited. She could hear Rob telling her to remain calm and Steven would get her down safe. She looked at the other platform only to see Jemma looking scared. She turned to look at the launching platform. She watched as Steven lowered himself and started towards her quickly, since both her and Steven's weight was pulling the line down even more than normal. He collided with her and bounced back a bit. Calmly he said, "Ericka, look at me." She turned and looked at him. "You are fine. You are going to sit on my lap and we will keep going. He scooted forward and said, "Ok now turn your body so you are facing me. Then wrap your legs around me. I won't let you fall."

She did as she was told and wrapped her legs around him while still holding onto her handle bars. She heard him groan and she pulled back and said, "Did I hurt you?"

He laughed, winking at her he said, "yes but not in the way you think."

Blushing she realized what he meant. But before she had time to think about it, he was giving her instructions again. "Ok now I need you to wrap one of your arms around me. Use the other hand to lift the handle off the line. That will give us a clear path to the other tree. Do you understand?"

She nodded and did as she was told. Rob and Mike were standing below them just in case and Steven said, "Rob, Ericka is going to drop her handle bars down so she can use both her hands to hold on." Nodding to Steven that he understood, Steven turned to Ericka, "Ok now grab one side of my handle bars and lift yours off the line. Now drop those handle bars and then grab the other side of my handle bars with your free hand. Be quick, we will start moving quickly."

Ericka looked into Steven's eyes and nodded. She grabbed one side of Stevens handle bars at the same time squeezing her legs around Steven for grip. He groaned again but she ignored him. She managed to lift her handle bars from the line and then dropped them as they started moving. She quickly grabbed the other side of Steven's handle bars.

He said, "Great. Now look at me. Keep your legs around me tight and hold on." They were moving and all she saw and felt was Steven. Until another pair of hands grabbed her waist. Steven said, "It's ok Ericka, Grant has you." She turned and looked over her shoulder and saw Grant and Charlie.

Grant said, "Ok Ericka take one arm from the handle and place it around my neck. You are not quite over the platform yet so I need to pull you toward me." He looked at Charlie and said, "You ready Charlie? On the count of three you're going to pull that rope." Charlie nodded at Grant. Grant turned back to Ericka and Steven and said, "Ok you two on the count of three, Charlie and I are going to pull you so you are over the platform completely. One, two, three." And with a strong tug on her waist, they were pulled over the platform into an odd shaped pile. Poor Grant took most of the weight pulling Ericka and Ericka pulling Steven. As Steven and Ericka rolled off Grant, they all tried to catch their breath. Grant untied the rope that was tied around his waist. That must have been the rope that Charlie pulled on.

Jemma and Rob were running toward them. Jemma practically tackled Ericka. "Are you ok?"

Laughing Ericka said, "I'm fine it's Grant and Steven you should be worried about. Steven had to hold me and Grant got the bottom of the pile."

Rob reached a hand down for Steven who took it and got up. Rob patted his shoulder and quietly said, "I'm sure you're hurting for other reasons." He said, chuckling, and walked away.

Ignoring Rob, Steven said, "I'm just glad it wasn't one of the boys that this happened to. I'm afraid of what would have happened."

They all started toward the picnic table, agreeing the zip line was closed for now. Trevor apologized and said he would look to see what had happened and get it fixed for the next time. Steven walked with Ericka, his hand lightly on the small of her back. All she really wanted to do was curl into him and breathe in his scent.

After getting everyone back to the house the kids started playing video games while the adults filled in Paige about the zip line. Seeing Mike's guard though, brought up the reason for his presence; Chad. No one knew if it was really Chad watching Ericka but she was almost positive. But what did it mean? Before he just plowed through the door and tried to take her. Now he was silently watching her and that was so much worse. She was on edge and needed to clear her head. Deciding she needed some air she went for a walk. What was she going to do? Move again? Why should she keep running when she had done nothing wrong? Besides she had a family now she didn't want to lose any of them. Then there was Steven. What were they doing? And what did it mean for their relationship and the family as a whole? If it went badly then she wouldn't feel comfortable around the Morgan family. But what if it turned out great? Steven has been such a great friend. She didn't want to mess that up, but felt that this could be something wonderful. To be in a relationship with one of your best friends, who now knew everything about you and liked you anyway, she thought it was worth the gamble. And let's face it, he invokes butterflies in her stomach whenever he is near.

The sound of crunching leaves behind her made her stop. Turning around she saw the man himself leaning against a tree watching her as if her thoughts had conjured his appearance. She smiled and made her way to the tree. "What are you up to out here sir?"

"Oh, I don't know. Felt like going on a walk with a beautiful woman. Are you free by chance?" He replied.

Laughing she wrapped her arm around his and pulled him to the path she was on. "So, we really didn't have a chance to talk about Chad or my special talent the other night. Both of us had other things on our minds." She said while waggling her eyebrows.

Smiling at her he said, "Well I am glad I know the whole story but I have to be honest and tell you I rather hope he shows up so I can beat the snot out of him."

"Oh, you are bad." She said and playfully smacked his shoulder. "I'm being serious now. With what we started the past few days, I really need to know what you think and if you are willing to stick around even if there is a crazy guy stalking me. You are too important to me as a friend and family, to risk messing this up. But I would love to explore where this may go with you."

He stopped and pulled her up against a tree. "I have to tell you I am glad that we started down this path and I look forward to exploring it with you. Had we been alone last night you would have known just how glad I was. You want to know if I'm willing to stick around even with a crazy person stalking you? Well, I'd like to see you try and get rid of me. I agree that our friendship is important though. But I know that friendship is why we are going to be fine. I have never wanted another woman as much as I want you right now Ericka. Do you think I could sneak behind your defenses and fight next to you? Because being next to you is where I want to be."

Steven kissed her then. Not a gentle loving kiss, but a fierce, passionate kiss. Ericka wound her hands up and into his hair, trying to pull him closer. Steven's hands were on her hips pulling her closer trying ease the ache they both had. Steven grabbed her thigh and lifted her leg so he could get closer still, causing her to buck against him. Drawing a groan from his chest.

"Christ," was all he could utter. He started grinding his hips against Ericka and she met him with each thrust. He let go of her leg and lifted her at her hips. "Wrap your legs around me."

She did as she was told and the instant connection almost sent them both over the edge. Using the tree as leverage he palmed one breast through her shirt. Making her throw her head back and moan. "Steven, please" She pulled his face up and kissed him deeply. Wanting to memorize everything about his mouth.

He tilted his hips up as he thrust and found the spot she liked as she moaned long and low. "Yes, Steven."

"Right there huh?" He replied, swinging his hips again and instantly pulling another moan from her.

Grabbing his face with both her hands, "Look at me Steven." Locking gazes, she moaned again. "Harder, don't hold back."

Eyes still locked, Steven pulled at her waist band and slid his hand inside her pants to her core. Thrusting two fingers inside her, he pulled a lusty cry from her lips. "Oh God, Steven." He increased the pressure and tempo. He was on the edge and he knew she was too. He could feel her muscles tightening around his fingers. Moving his thumb up to find her nub of pleasure, he pressed and rubbed his thumb against her nub and brought on her climax. Moaning his name, she closed her eyes and rode the waves. She opened her eyes and looked at Steven. "What about you?"

Putting her feet on the ground Ericka used the tree to steady herself. She had not expected this when she thought about talking to Steven about them, but she should have. She wasn't willing to take all the pleasure herself though, and she had a good idea of what was to happen since it was playing out like in her dream. Looking around to make sure they hadn't attracted attention, she pulled him against the tree, taking his place. Putting her hands on his chest she kissed him, long and slow, while moving her hands down to the bulge of his pants and rubbing it up and down. Putting his head back against the tree, he groaned from deep in his chest. Ericka's fingers played along the band of his pants before unbuttoning his pants. Reaching inside his boxers she wrapped her hand around him and lightly squeezed. "Christ" he hissed while sucking in air sharply into his lungs. Ericka's other hand played with Steven's pants and boxers slowly giving her more room to play. Before Steven knew what was happening, Ericka was on her knees. With her hand still wrapped around him, she licked the rounded tip and played with it before taking him into her mouth. "Oh God" he said as she sucked and licked and played with him all while stroking him and cupping his balls.

He had never felt such pleasure in his life. She was like a siren and everything she touched turned into pleasure. She started taking him deeper and he wound his hands into her hair. He was going to explode any minute. He tried to pull her up but she just looked at him and smiled taking him deeper still, while gently squeezing the base of his cock. And he lost it. Thrusting into her mouth now he was unaware of anything other than Ericka and her talented mouth. He tried to pull out but she grabbed his ass and held him there. Looking into her eyes he thrust once more and, with an explosion, he came hard and fast. He had never felt anything like that; ever. As he floated down from the stratosphere he thought, Mine. She is mine. Looking down into Ericka's face, she smiled at him, wiped her mouth and pulled up his boxers and pants. Still panting, Steven couldn't talk. He didn't know what to say after something like that. He pulled her to him and he kissed her gently. Showing her just how much he cared about her. Placing his forehead to hers all he could say was, "Wow". Making them both laugh out loud.

So many emotions and thoughts flying around his mind, but he needed to tell her. "Ericka, I want you. I want us to take this journey. I want to protect you and fight beside you. I want to explore more of what just happened." She laughed and rested her head on his chest. "I don't know how to explain it, but this feels like it was supposed to happen all along. That we were made for each other."

Looking up she placed both hands on his cheeks. "I don't know what this is between us. I have never felt this way before, so I'm hesitant to name it, but I want to explore it with you Steven." She turned to go and stopped. "By the way, this what just happened, yah that was my dream last night. I told you it would happen this trip."

Chuckling he wrapped his arms around her and she wrapped hers around him as they headed back to the house. There would be lots of looks, grinning and questions they would need to face, but they would face them together.

Chapter 7

The next day while getting coffee, Paige sat down next to Ericka and said, "We have family pictures today, and we would like you to be in them Ericka."

Ericka looked up at Paige and swallowed. She had never been in family pictures before. She said, "I don't know. You don't need me in your pictures."

Paige picked up her hands in hers, "You and I both know you are part of this family, and a part of me thinks that may end up being a permanent thing sooner than you realize."

Ericka searched her eyes. "You would be ok with that? I know I don't have much other than a horrible history. And Steven and I are still not even sure what's happening between us yet. I would hate for you to think I'm trying to get him to marry me."

Paige laughed. "You should have seen both your faces last night when you came back from your walk. You both may be dragging your feet to name this, but the entire family already knows and is thrilled, by the way." She placed her hand on Ericka's cheek and said, "I will never be able to repay you for the help you gave to Jemma with Clint. I was not able to step in but you were and I shudder to think what would have happened to my baby without you." Wiping her cheek she said, "Bottom line no matter what happens with Steven, you are already a part of this family; an essential part."

Ericka was crying freely now. "I've never really had a family before. I had my aunt and uncle but they were older and left me on my own a lot of the time." Wiping her face, she threw her arms around Paige and hugged her. Paige had stepped into the role of mom as soon as they met. Closing her eyes, she whispered into her ear she said, "Thank you, mom, for everything."

She felt hands on her shoulder and before she knew it, she was being turned into another hug, this time by Trevor. "Ever since the day we met you, you have been part of our family in our thoughts and our hearts."

She was a mess now. Not able to speak she was turned into yet another hug. "We love you, Ericka. You have been a sister in my heart from the moment you reached out to me on campus. You fought for me when I couldn't fight for myself and watched over me like a big sister would." Pulling back, she looked into Jemma's face.

"You will never know how much this means to me." Ericka whispered. Drying her eyes she laughed and said, "But seriously if you wanted me in your pictures, you probably should not have turned me into a watering pot."

They all laughed at that. Turning to head into bathroom, she saw Steven standing there leaning against the door. His eyes were shiny, but he smiled and winked at her. She walked past him and took his arm and pulled him with her down the hall where she wrapped her arms around him and he held her while she finished crying her unshed tears.

*   *   *   *   *   *   *   *

When Steven and Jemma had walked into the kitchen and saw Ericka hugging their mom and dad pulling her into another embrace. He had worried at first that something had happened, but then he heard his dad tell her she was part of the family. He got choked up and stayed by the door while Jemma went to Ericka. His parents were right though, she was part of the family with or without him in the picture. But when she smiled at him, he had almost let the tears that were building go, but she pulled him down the hall and just held him. She needed his strength and she would always have it no matter what. He stroked her hair and whispered endearments to her. He wiped his cheek as a few tears managed to escape his eyes. "Ericka, love, we need to get cold compresses on your eyes so they are not swollen for the pictures." Came his mom's voice from down the hall. They both turned to look at her and she smiled at them then walked back into the kitchen.

Reaching up on tip toe she leaned in and kissed him. The most tender and loving kiss he had ever had in his life. It wasn't about sex or lust, it was about love and souls that were meant to be together, finally coming together. He cupped her cheeks and looked into her eyes. And in that moment, he knew. He knew that he loved her and that he had always loved her. He no longer felt lost when he was with her, he felt whole. Clearing his throat he said, "Are you ok?"

"I am now." She replied and kissed him quickly once more and left down the hall to find Paige.

*   *   *   *   *   *   *   *

Later that day, they met their photographer and had the family portraits done. Jemma and Rob had theirs done as well. In all the pictures Ericka was right by Steven and he always had a hand on her somehow. A hand on her back, her hip or just holding her hand. It was a really special day. Back at the house everyone just relaxed. Ericka was out on the porch swing watching the sun set, thinking about how very blessed she was with the Morgan family. All because someone had reached out to her in her time of need, she had done the same to Jemma. She could honestly say she had never been happier than she was at this very moment. Hearing the screen door open she turned to see Steven. "Mind if I join you?" he asked.

Patting the space next to her she said, "Please do."

Sitting down next to her, she took his arm, lifted it and snuggled into him. He pulled her closer and she said, "Perfect. Would you just hold me while we watch the sun set?"

He kissed the top of her head and said, "It would be my pleasure."

It was one of those moments that she knew she would always look back on and know that she had found where she belonged. Looking up at Steven she knew then that she was in love with him and that she probably had been from day one. She wrapped her other arm around his stomach and he looked down at her and kissed her forehead. She smiled and he kissed the tip of her nose. She giggled and he covered her mouth with his, in a kiss that made her toes curl in her shoes. "I love the sound of your giggle." He whispered against her lips, which made her giggle even more.

"Oh hush" she playfully swatted him.

"Ok you don't want me to talk about your giggles. Well, let me tell you about another sound you make that I can't get enough of."

She looked up into his eyes and saw a flame of desire there. His eyes were dilated to where you could barely see the green. Playing along she said, "Oh really? I have other sounds I make?"

He bent down and nipped her neck, making her gasp. "That's one of the sounds," he murmured.

"Really?" she said, "I'm not sure I really heard a sound." She said playfully.

He bent down again and sucked in her ear lobe and nibbled on it, causing her to gasp again. "Ok I heard it that time." She panted.

"Hmm," was his reply. He moved to her jaw line and placed kisses along toward her mouth. Skipping over her mouth and moving down to her collarbone, causing her to moan in frustration. She wanted to kiss him, but he was playing with her now. "That's another sound I like to hear from you," he said while tracing her collarbone with his tongue.

He pulled her onto his lap and ran a hand down her side toying with the underside of her breast but not stopping.

His hand mapped her body down to her hip where he grabbed her and pulled her closer. Sliding his hand from her hip he cupped her bottom and gently massaged the perfect globe, making her moan for a completely different reason. Smiling down on her he said, "There; that's the sound I was looking for." And he covered her mouth with his, tightening his grip on Ericka's bottom and she deepened the kiss.

There was laughter coming from the living room toward the door. This time Steven groaned. He didn't want to stop this game with Ericka. She giggled again and said, "I'm not the only one that makes wonderful sounds." She gave him a quick kiss and slid off his lap back onto the swing and tucked under his arm.

Steven chuckled, "Touché, my dear."

Jemma came out and looked at them and smiled. "We were just talking about having an outing tomorrow if you two are up for it."

They looked at each other and smiled. "Of course. Where are we going?" Steven replied.

"Well since Ericka hasn't been up here before, we thought a trip to the Multnomah falls would be fun. There are a couple great hikes there or we can just hang out at the falls." Jemma said.

Sitting up quickly she asked, "Really? That is one place I have always seen in pictures and wanted to visit." Ericka said turning to Steven.

*   *   *   *   *   *   *   *

At that moment when he looked into her eyes, he vowed to always try to have that look in her eyes. Her eyes were bright and full with such a shining light you knew no darkness could penetrate it. "I'd love to go to Multnomah falls. I can take you up to the bridge and even show you some of the side falls if you're up for a hike."

With that settled they planned for late morning early afternoon so they could have lunch at the restaurant there at the falls. Ericka was excited and couldn't wait. She said she had seen the falls so many times in pictures but had never made it this far north in her travels to visit. It was a great way to end their trip to the Morgan Family home.

That evening they decided to play board games. While the ladies were setting up the games, Trevor pulled all the men outside. "I wanted to give you all an update on the harness for the zipline."

They followed him outside to the patio where he explained, "After I looked at the harness, I knew something was off. The rope that broke was almost new. So, I looked

113

closer and it appears someone cut through most of the rope and left enough that after being used a couple times it pulled the rest through." He walked over to where Steven was standing. "I know Ericka is having troubles with her ex so I wanted to let you know. Your instincts are probably correct. You all need to keep an eye on each other today." He looked around at all the men. "Now let's not ruin your mom's last night. Let's get in there and try and have some fun." He smacked Steven's back and then Grant's back on his way inside.

Everyone was gathered around the dining room table ready to play. Steven sat next to Ericka while Rob took Erin duty and put her down for Jemma. Steven didn't know how he was going to fake not being worried, but by the end of the first round everyone was laughing and having a great time. They played board games until the wee hours of the morning. Jemma called a break at 11 so the boys could be put to bed. Charlie decided to turn in too, so he would be ready for the hike tomorrow. Shortly after the boys went to bed, Paige and Trevor threw in the towel in favor of their bed. So, it was just the three couples still playing and having a wonderful time. Steven was getting picked on due to the beautiful lady sitting next to him. But he didn't care one bit. He rather loved the fact that everyone was already treating them as couple. At three am, Erin woke up for her mid night snack.

They could hear her on the monitor. Rob rose with Jemma and said, "That's our que. I don't want her waking up the house, because she will, trust me, if she doesn't get her snack."

Everyone laughed and Grant said, "sounds like her mother." Which, caused another round of laughter.

Since the game was breaking up, they all decided it was a good time to call it a night. Grant and Cindy followed Jemma and Rob upstairs. And Ericka pulled Steven to her room. Pushing him inside, she locked the door and reached down for her shirt and pulled it over her head. Throwing it to the floor she started toward Steven who was still getting his footing after being pushed into the room. Steven just watched her as she kicked her shoes off and slowly pulled down her shorts. Soon she was standing in front of him with only a bra and panties on. Swallowing hard, Steven said, "Ericka." She placed her finger against his lips stopping him from protesting. She reached out and grabbed the bottom of his shirt dragging it over his head and throwing it on the floor with Ericka's clothes.

She traced his ribs with a finger and ran her fingers through the hair on his chest pausing to rub his nipple between her finger and thumb, making him groan. He reached out for her hips pulling her to him and he kissed her. Coming up for air he said, "Ericka I may not be able to stop."

Smiling she said "I certainly hope you don't stop." And with that comment he grabbed her and tossed her onto the bed.

He took off his shoes and pants, only his boxers remained. He prowled to the bed flexing his arm muscles as he went. He was so wound up he hoped he would be able to last. Before he got into the bed, Ericka knelt on the bed and unhooked her bra. Letting it fall, she looked at Steven. His breath caught and his mouth went dry. "You are stunning Ericka."

Standing she pushed him onto the bed on his back. Slowly she shimmied out of her panties and she stood there gloriously in not a stitch of clothing. Sitting up he pulled her between his legs, which gave him the perfect height for drawing a pert nipple into his mouth causing her to moan and legs to go weak. He reached out and wrapped an arm around her bottom to hold her in place. Her hand dove into his hair to hold him in place while she arched into his mouth. Steven reached down and stroked the outside of her leg to her knee, then retracing his path on the inside of her thigh. Teasing her, he skipped over her core and followed the same course on the other leg at the same time switching breasts. Soon his hand was back at the apex between her thighs and he cupped her mound causing her to buck into his hand. Playing with her folds, he found her wet and ready for him. Pulling away from her breast he looked up into her eyes.

She grabbed his face in her hands and staring into his eyes said, "I am yours Steven. Only yours. I love you."

Steven's throat got tight and pulled her to his lap and pressed his forehead to hers. "I love you too Ericka. I have a feeling I always have." And he took her mouth with his, claiming it as his own.

Breaking the kiss, Ericka said, "Make me yours Steven. I need you inside of me."

He rolled her onto her back and kissed his way down her neck to the valley between her breasts. "Man, you have the best body." He took a breast in each hand and massaged them and licked the pert nipples into hardened peaks.

Releasing her breasts his hand traveled down to the apex between her thighs and he thrust two fingers inside of her causing her to groan while holding onto his shoulders. "Yes, my love" he whispered. He could feel she was on the edge, so he slowed down and pulled away with a cry of disapproval coming from her.

Chuckling he said, "I'll be right there."

Grabbing a condom from his jeans, he took off his boxers and put it on. When he climbed back up on the bed, she was ready and pulled him to her and with one thrust he was seated deeply within her causing them both to moan out loud. It was a good thing they were downstairs and everyone else was upstairs. She wrapped her legs around him allowing him to go even deeper. He withdrew and thrust back into her to a rhythm that she met thrust for thrust. He took one of her legs and lifted it to his shoulder, turning to kiss her knee he thrust deeper into her. Panting she locked gazes with him and said, "harder Steven, don't hold back."

Groaning with pleasure he said, "you really are going to be the death of me."

He started pounding into her, causing her moans to get louder and longer. "That's it my love, let go for me. I'll catch you." He murmured. Letting her leg go he bent down and took her mouth with his as she climaxed, pulling him along with her over that sweet edge until they were both riding the waves back down to earth.

Collapsing on top of Ericka, Steven couldn't breathe. Never before had someone touched his very soul like Ericka had. He raised himself up onto his elbows and looked down into her face. She was smiling up at him and stroked his cheeks. "I have never felt like that before. Tell me it was as special for you as it was for me." She shyly asked.

He rolled off to the side and took her with him. Kissing her temple, he choked out "Words cannot describe what just happened and how much it meant to me. And no, I have never felt that way either. You are mine Ericka."

She gave him a sleepy grin and said, "Always." Before drifting to sleep.

Steven laid there stroking her back and watching her sleep. He was not going to survive being apart from this woman. But he really couldn't ask her to marry him with the whole Chad situation still up in the air. As he drifted to sleep, he decided she would not be going back to Los Angeles alone. She was his now and he was hers.

*   *   *   *   *   *   *   *

It had taken longer than he wanted to get to Oregon and find where the Morgan's lived. But luckily, he was fortunate enough to be able to hear about the zipline outing. He didn't have much trouble finding the harnesses in the shed. He sliced almost all the way through one seat and used some wax and gum to gum up the gear wheel on the bars. He really hoped that guy, Steven, would be the one to fall. But he would be happy just to cause problems. The new guard that showed up that same day was giving him trouble though. He wasn't able to get close to the house as often to listen. That really threw a kink in his plan. Tonight, however he was able to hear the old man tell the men about his sabotage of the harness. Good. They should be scared. Especially Steven. Too bad for that guard otherwise he'd try and grab Annie during the night. She was the only one downstairs. Foolish of them to leave her alone like that.

He snuck over to where the window was to her room. The light was off but there was noise coming from the room. As he got closer, he heard the sounds of pleasure coming from window and all he saw was red. He was going to kill him. That was all there was too it. The sound of the front door opening and closing made him abandon his post for the woods. The guard was making his rounds again. As he quietly moved in the shadows, he pictured the moment he would kill Steven. Hiking back to his truck he settled in for the night. The anger keeping him awake and as the night progressed, his anger simmered. He was going to have to bide his time.

Chapter 8

The morning came bright and early and so did the knock at Ericka's door. They both sat up and looked at each other. "Crap we fell asleep." They said at the same time. The door was knocked on again and they heard Rob, "Steven, Jemma is distracting your mom, grab your clothes and high tail it upstairs."

Jumping out of the bed, Steven grabbed his boxers and threw on his t-shirt. Looking back at Ericka, all he wanted to do was jump back in that bed and ravage her some more. "Can you try to not look so sexy please? I'm having a hard enough time pulling myself away from you already." She laughed and let the sheet fall giving him a glorious view of her breasts. Growling he stalked back to her and grabbing the back of her head kissed her hard. Leaving them both panting for air.

She pushed at him laughing, "Go before it's too late."

Planting another, quicker kiss, he grabbed his shoes, stopping at the door, "this isn't over love. You need to prepare yourself." He grinned at her over his shoulder.

Slowly he opened the door and slid outside, pulling the door closed behind him. He was heading up the stairs when he heard a cough at the bottom of the stairs. He turned and found Rob barely keeping it together. Laughing he said, "Hurry they are almost done in the kitchen."

He didn't need to tell him twice, he all but sprinted to his room and quietly slid inside. Bracing himself against the door, he smiled. It was going to be hard not to touch her or smile like a fool today. Gathering his things, he walked to the bathroom to get ready for the day. He had just finished shaving when there was a knock on the door. "Steven is that you? I knocked on your door but didn't get an answer." Thank goodness for Rob.

"Yah Mom, I'm almost done." He lied. He hadn't even gotten in the shower yet.

"Ok we will be leaving in about 45 minutes or so for the falls. So be quick." She responded.

Taking the quickest shower of his life he finished getting ready and headed downstairs to grab something to eat quickly before they left. He walked into the kitchen and found Rob, Jemma and Ericka at the table. Ericka looked up and blushed prettily and looked back down at her plate. He smiled at Rob who smiled knowingly back at him. Jemma was trying to keep her cool but she was smiling as well.

"Good morning, everyone," Steven said. "I hope I'm not making the caravan late."

"Not at all," Rob said. "The other van just left. Your Dad isn't able to go with us, something came up at work. And your mom is staying with Erin. So, it's the four of us in the car."

Grabbing a coffee mug, he poured himself a cup of coffee. "Great." Sitting in the chair next to Ericka, he looked at her over his coffee mug. She was still blushing and staring at her food. He set down his coffee and grabbed a bagel and took a bite and dropped his hand into his lap. Slowly he reached over and grabbed Ericka's knee, causing her to jump. She turned and looked at him while Jemma and Rob busted out laughing.

Ericka started laughing and said, "Really? You're going to grab my knee after what happened this morning?"

Jemma snorted, "What exactly happened this morning?"

It was Rob's turn to snort, "If you don't know by now, we may need to stay behind too." Earning himself a smack from Jemma.

Steven laughed. "I'm sorry I scared you, but I'm not hiding anything about us. I hope you are ok with that."

Exhaling she said, "I'm more than fine with not hiding, it's the getting caught sleeping with the son of the hosts in their craft room that I have an issue with." Which made everyone bust out laughing.

Taking a drink of his coffee, Rob said, "Don't worry. We are the only ones who know. Your mom was knocking on your door Steven and when you didn't answer I had my suspicions."

"Well thank you then," Ericka said. "It's probably a good thing we are leaving tomorrow."

"Don't worry about my parents," Jemma said, "Ask Rob about the conversation Mom had with him telling him I needed to sleep with him."

Rob snorted, "That was a different situation entirely. But yes, I was a little caught off guard by that conversation."

Standing Ericka said, "Let's get this party started. I have waited a long time to see these falls, and we can talk awkward conversations on the road."

"Well said Ericka," Jemma stood. Let me go check on Erin quickly and meet you all in the car."

Standing and taking Ericka's hand in his, he pulled Ericka out the door and toward the car. "Let's hurry so we can sit in the back." He said while laughing and running to the car. He pinned her to the trunk and nuzzled her neck.

"Steven, your parents are still here and can probably see us." Ericka protested.

"I told you I'm not going to hide you. You are too precious and important to be a secret." He retorted then nipped her ear lobe.

A loud crash came from the shed. They both turned to see what it was but saw nothing. Turning back to Steven, Ericka said, "Fine, just get in the car before you start to nibble on me then." She responded.

"With pleasure my love." He opened the door for her and she slid in.

*   *   *   *   *   *   *   *

This was going to take some getting used to. She never had anyone call her a term of endearment before. She buckled and turned to Steven. "I know you don't want to hide about us and I agree with you, but just take it slow with me, ok? I don't have the best track record and I'm not used to the endearments and attention. I am used to only having myself to worry about. Not that I'm worried. It's just..."

He brushed the back of his knuckles across her cheek. "I know. We have each been alone for a long time. I will try and curb my enthusiasm. But I'm not going to pretend there is nothing going on between us either. Ok."

"Agreed." She said as she snuggled against him ready for the drive.

"There is something we need to talk about though, and it's a good thing it's just us with Rob and Jemma. We need to talk about Chad and what we are going to do. I'm supposed to go home tomorrow and I'll be honest with you Steven, the thought of going back by myself, scares the hell out of me."

He pulled her closer to him and kissed the top of her head. "That's not going to happen. We will talk to Rob and Jemma and see what they think we should do. Unfortunately, they have a bit more knowledge and experience with crazy people."

Ericka giggled into his chest. "Ma'am, I do believe I told you what happens when you giggle." He said as he pressed her into the seat. He had just kissed her when the doors opened.

"Ugh, get a room will ya?" Rob said while Jemma laughed.

"We did have one but you kicked us out." Ericka said.

"Oh, good one." Jemma said laughing.

They pulled out of the drive and headed to the falls. "We need to chat with you two," Steven said. "You guys are all leaving tomorrow and I don't want Ericka going back to her place by herself. What do you suggest we do about Chad?"

They talked about the situation all the way to the falls and had come up with a plan, kind of. But decided to talk more later tonight as they were almost to the falls now. Steven was on the phone with his travel agent booking a ticket on Ericka's flight tomorrow, when they pulled up to the falls. Ericka opened the door and stood there quietly watching the falls. Steven noticed how quiet she was and he walked over and took her hand in his while he finished his call.

Quietly she looked at Steven with a tear rolling down her face and said, "It's absolutely breathtaking. I honestly never thought I would make it here." Wiping her tears away with his thumbs he kissed her forehead and pulled her toward the falls.

Just as they came around the little store, they heard a high-pitched squeal, "Momma." Tom came flying at Jemma, talking a mile a minute. "Uncle Grant said I couldn't go on the bridge until you got here. Can we go now?"

Jemma looked and Grant and said, "Thank you. I'm sure he has been pestering you."

Cindy came over and hugged Tom from behind. "Not at all, we've been trying to figure out if there is anything hiding behind the water fall. Which has kept all three of the boys busy."

Nodding in agreement, Tom looked at Jemma, "Can we go up there now?"

Looking around Jemma saw everyone was there and so they made their way up the steps to the stone bridge. You could feel the spray from the water fall. The trail leading up to the bridge wasn't very strenuous, but there were other trails that branched off the main trail that were challenging. After discussing it they decided to do a harder hike on another visit. Grant told the boys about other waterfalls off the other trails but nothing compared to Multnomah. Once on the bridge, the boys carefully looked over the rail with Rob and Grant's help. You couldn't really see clearly, since the falls were churning the water making white tipped waves. The falls are actually comprised of one waterfall, falling in two tiers. The main water fall fell to the back of the bridge and then ran underneath the bridge to the next tier to the lower part, where they had just come from. From there it flowed on down to the Columbia River.

They walked along the main trail so they could try and see behind the curtain of water, but they couldn't. The stone bridge was wet from the spray off the falls, and everyone was wet. They decided to head back down and find out about the restaurant. Ericka wanted a few moments of quiet to just take in the magnificent site of the falls. Along the trail there were places to sit, formed from rock or wood. The group headed down to the main observation deck. Ericka sat and just watched the water fall. Closing her eyes, she felt the mixture of heat from the sun and spray from the water fall. She sat there just soaking up the beauty that this place held. She loved the sound of the water fall. She felt a sense of peace within her as she opened her eyes and watched the water fall. She knew she still had Chad to deal with but she would not let him take this moment from her. She knew she was loved by Steven and knew she belonged to a family, the Morgan family. Nothing could ever change that no matter how he tried. She knew Steven was there before she felt him sit down next to her. "It's just so beautiful," she said turning toward him and looked into his eyes, which were filled with love.

"Not as beautiful as you sitting there with your face tilted up toward the sun and with the waterfall behind you. I may have snuck a picture with my phone."

He put his arm around her and pulled her close. She pulled out her phone and said, "Let's take a picture together showing we were here together." She snapped a selfie of her and Steven with the falls in the back ground. She also took a picture of just Steven.

They sat there quietly for a few more minutes before Steven kissed her temple and said, "You don't have to face him alone this time Ericka. I will be there at your side ready to protect you."

She knew he wouldn't leave her. And she was so relieved she didn't have to face Chad alone this time. They still needed to finalize the plan though. That would be done later tonight after the kiddos were in bed. Now it was time to join the rest of their group and enjoy their last day in Oregon. They gathered and took a group photo then set out to explore.

The day flew by but soon it was time for everyone to talk about the plan. This was something they all needed to agree on as it affected more than just Ericka now. That evening everyone sat down to discuss the options for Ericka. They decided that Steven, Rob and Ericka would fly to LA and Jemma and the kids would fly on to Hawaii with Mike and his guard while Rob and Steven helped pack up Ericka. It was time to move again. Rob was sending Mike and the body guard with Jemma and the kids since he wouldn't be with them. He wasn't taking any chances with Jemma again and Ericka didn't blame him one bit. It was decided that Ericka would head to Jemma's and stay in one of the cabins until they could figure out a better plan. But they had to move Ericka quickly.

Trevor decided then that it was time the ladies knew about the harness and proceeded to fill them in on the details about the harness which caused an uproar. Shocked to hear about the harness, Ericka was just beside herself. Tears ran freely down her face. She looked around the room at all the people she truly loved and knew she was the cause of harm here. It could have been any of the family, especially the children, when that harness snapped. She stood and the room got quiet.

"I never meant for any of you to get hurt or caught up in this crazy mess that I call my life. I am so glad it was me and not one of you that the harness broke. I would never forgive myself if any of you were to get hurt because of me. I think I will reschedule my flight and head out tonight. Rob, you go home with Jemma. I will send my new address once I get settled somewhere probably off the grid." The group all started to object and she held up her hand. "I have dealt with this longer than I care to admit but I've gotten quite good at disappearing. I am so sorry I brought this to your home." Ericka cried. And ran to her room.

Everyone was quiet as they watched Ericka run down the hall. "Oh, that poor girl. Will she ever feel safe and not alone?" Paige cried. Trevor went to her and wrapped her in his arms.

Steven looked at Jemma who said, "We need to talk to her Steven. She can't do this alone this time. I am worried that since he has changed his tactics and followed her here that she is in extreme danger this time." Steven nodded his agreement and they walked to Ericka's room.

Jemma knocked on her door. "Ericka. It's me and Steven. Can we come in?"

All they heard was Ericka crying. "I'm not letting you go through this alone Ericka. So, whether you want me in there or not, I'm coming in." Steven said.

He opened the door and they found Ericka sitting on the floor, her head between her knees sobbing. Steven went to and pulled her onto his lap. Jemma sat on the bed and rubbed her back. "You aren't alone anymore Ericka. You are the strongest woman I know, but you do not have to shoulder this yourself. And this isn't your fault." Jemma reassured her.

"How can I let you all risk being my friend? If he is willing to hurt innocent children, anyone around me is not safe." Ericka cried and turned her head into Steven's chest.

"Ericka. Look at me." Steven said softly. He tipped her chin up so she would look at him. "I am not leaving your side. No matter how much you wish it, I will stalk you myself to make sure you are safe. The plan for everyone to go to Hawaii is the safest course. We both know that Rob can handle himself but you are the one with the bullseye on her back. And if it is Chad who cut the harness, he has probably seen us together too. It is safer if we stay together." He leaned in and put his forehead on hers. "I can't lose you now." He whispered.

Ericka cupped his cheek and stared into his eyes and saw the love and the truth of those words in his eyes. She cupped his other cheek with her free hand and kissed him. "I am a selfish person to willingly put you in harm's way, just so I won't be by myself." She whispered back.

They both looked up at click of the door. Jemma had snuck out of the room so they could discuss this. Ericka smiled and said, "I didn't even hear her get up."

Steven smiled. "Does that smile mean you are going to let us help you?" He searched her eyes for the answer. She nodded and he kissed her. Not a gentle kiss but a kiss to claim her and remind her that she was not alone. He turned her so she would straddle him and pulled her closer.

She could not get close enough to Steven. Try as she might, she could not. She wound her hands in his hair and pulled him back, "I need you, Steven."

He kissed her and grabbed her shirt and lifted it up over her head. He caressed her arms and up to her neck to finally cupping her cheeks. "Are you sure?" he asked.

Ericka stood and dropped her pants and panties and sat back down on Steven's lap. "Yes." She reached down and undid his pants, while he took off his shirt. He started to get up but Ericka wouldn't let him. Kneeling she helped his slide out of his pants and in one move took all of Steven into her core, making him throw his head back and groan. Ericka placed her hand on his shoulder and rose and fell to the rhythm that would drown out all the loneliness she felt. She was no longer alone. Throwing her head back she closed her eyes and moaned as Steven took her breast in his mouth. "There is the sound I love." Steven said. "Take me. Take everything you need."

Ericka looked down and into his eyes and kissed him slowly, passionately. She needed him. And he was giving himself to her. Eyes locked she increased her pace and drove harder. She needed to fill the broken piece of her heart and Steven was the remedy. "Steven, I..." The waves of her release started and she threw her head back and moaned low and long.

"Ericka." Was all Steven could get out and he followed her over into the bliss. She started slowing down and rode out the last of the waves. She collapsed on top of Steven and he smiled and rubbed her back. They sat there holding each other for a while. Neither wanted to say a word or this spell might break. Deciding they better dress before a child walked in, they quietly pulled themselves together. Siting on the floor against the wall they held hands and just absorbed this feeling that this was right. They were meant to be together. Ericka laid her head against his arm and finally broke the silence. "I would never forgive myself if anything happened to your family." She whispered.

"Our family." Steven corrected her. "And you need to know that anyone in that room would gladly fight in your corner with you and even for you if you would just let them help you."

"I know. It's just I have been having to deal with this by myself for so long it is hard to accept help." She said sadly. "But I need help. I can't keep doing this. It is not a life I would wish on my worst enemy." She looked up and said, "Think I should go back out there and apologize?"

"No. I think you should go back out there and tell them you need and accept their help." He said truthfully. "You have nothing to apologize for but know this, mom will be crying and will probably wrap you up in her arms." He laughed.

"Ok. How do I look?" she asked.

"Ravishing. But I'll try and control myself." He replied.

Together they walked back out to the front room and before Ericka could say a word, Paige wrapped her arms around her. "You are my daughter, Ericka. Please let us help you."

As the tears fell, Ericka nodded her agreement. "I'm scared and I need help." Ericka whispered. Only Paige, Jemma and Steven heard her. Paige started sobbing and tightened her hold.

"I know you are scared, sweetheart. You would be a fool otherwise." Paige pulled back and said, "We will get through this together."

Ericka turned to the rest of the room and said, "Thank you for helping me. I really am grateful."

They all sat down and went over the plan again, now that they all knew Chad had been there.

Chapter 9

Trevor and Paige took the group to the airport while getting promises to return and to call with updates from each group. They all boarded the plane and once again, Ericka was able to have some time to herself to think. This time it was more about the plan and Chad than the new relationship with Steven. But before she knew it, they were landing in Los Angeles.

Seeing Jemma, Mike and everyone else safely onto their flight they grabbed their luggage and headed to Ericka's house. Everything looked normal and nothing out of place. They decided to grab boxes and a storage unit the next day and start packing then. It had been a long day and everyone was beat. Rob left Steven and Ericka to themselves and went to bed. Turning to look up at Steven, Ericka laughed and said, "Geez if this isn't weird, I don't know what is. I'm just not sure what to do with myself. Do I throw myself at you? Cuddle with you? Or just wait until this whole Chad situation is resolved?"

Steven wrapped his arms around her and pinned her to the couch saying, "We are not waiting on anything, and if I have a vote, I'd take throwing yourself at me personally."

They both laughed and he pulled her back up. It was just the tension release they needed. Ericka stood up and decided to check her messages while grabbing a drink. The first two were telemarketers, one was about school and then there was a call from Grace.

"Ericka, if you are listening to this message, please be careful. I found out that Chad was fired and that he has been telling people he is coming for you and that he was going to go get his wife back. He has lost it Ericka. Please, please be careful." Click.

Steven was by Ericka's side as soon as he heard Chad's name. "Well, it seems your instincts were correct. But what we need to know is when he left and if he knew where to look?"

Steven walked to Rob's door and knocked. He came out and they listened to it again. Rob watched Ericka's face. She was getting paler by the second. "I think, Ericka, that you should head to the island. Let Steven and I get everything settled here."

Steven shook his head. "Where she goes, I go. I am not letting her out of my sight Rob. We just need to be quick and get this done."

139

Ericka promised to call Grace in the morning to see if there were any details she could find out. They needed all the information they could get so they could be prepared.

Rob went back to bed and Ericka and Steven followed shortly after. A couple hours later, after tossing and turning, Ericka got up and went to grab a drink. Walking to the kitchen she saw a light on under Steven's door. She knocked and asked if he was ok. He opened the door with just his boxers on. Ericka looked at him and drank in the sight of him. Man, he was gorgeous with his tousled hair, loose boxers, and no shirt. She looked from top to bottom. When she looked at his feet, he wiggled his toes, breaking the trance she was in. Laughing he asked, "look all you want."

She smiled and said, "I'd rather taste if you don't mind." And she pushed him lightly back into his room. Now her mouth was dry for another reason altogether. She needed to feel alive and loved. Kissing him firmly she pulled back and said, "Well you did say you'd pick me throwing myself at you. I would have to agree with that choice. That is if you don't mind."

Laughing Steven, laid on the bed and said, "I am yours to do with as you please, my dear. Have your way with me. You will get no objections from me."

Just as Ericka was about climb on to the bed, there was a loud banging at the front door. Steven jumped up and they both ran into the hall bumping into Rob. They all looked at each other. Rob grabbed Ericka and put her behind Steven and he went to the door. Looking out the peep hole he saw nothing. He turned and looked at Ericka, "do you get doorbell ditchers here?"

Shaking her head, she pressed her forehead into Steven's back and let a whimper come out. Steven reached behind him and pulled her under his arm. She was tucked up in his chest, when Rob opened the door. No one was there, but someone had been there. There was a bouquet of flowers but the tops of the flowers were gone. It was just the stems and leaves. Rob picked it up and shut the door, locking all five locks. There was a card with the stems and Rob pulled it out, looked at it and handed it to Ericka.

On the front had her old name *'Annie'* written on it and on the back *'I will always find you'*. Dropping the card, she turned into Steven's chest and buried her face in her hands and sobbed. Steven held her rubbing her back trying to comfort her, but how does one comfort something like this.

Steven looked to Rob who was watching the scene unfold. "She shouldn't be alone after this Steven. You need to stay with her. I also think that we need to rethink our plan.

He knows we are back and no matter where she moves, he will follow her. I think for now we should get one of those POD storage containers and fill it with her stuff and send it to your parents' house until we can come up with our next move."

Steven nodded and placed his hand on her cheeks. "What do you think Ericka? Are you ok with that?"

Whispering she said, "I don't care, just don't leave me Steven." And she buried her face in his chest.

"Never." Steven whispered in her ear. Nodding to Rob he steered Ericka to her room. He would stay with her tonight and make sure she was safe and cared for. If he didn't know any better, he would have sworn Chad was watching him and Ericka and choose that moment to pound on the door.

Steven held Ericka in his arms all night. They both slept poorly but at least they were together. Morning came and brought all kinds of questions. Ericka called and talked to Grace. They did find out that he was driving a beat-up brown truck. Grace didn't have any additional information though. Ericka reassured Grace that she had help and they were making a plan. She told her about the flowers and the note. "Ericka I am really afraid for you this time. He has completely lost touch with reality. I am afraid of what he will do if he gets a hold of you. Please make sure your friends have my number so someone can keep me updated." Ericka agreed and told her she would call her once she was settled to let her know where.

Rob called and ordered a Pod to be delivered the next day and left to grab boxes and supplies. Ericka was not stepping foot out of the apartment until it was time to leave. Ericka went to the room Steven had been staying in and stripped the beds, went through the closet, and started making piles on the bed in preparation of Rob returning with boxes. She wanted to get at least two rooms packed today. Steven ordered food and they got to work. Rob returned and wrapped the dressers and night stands to secure the drawers while Ericka filled the boxes. They moved on to Rob's bedroom and repeated the process except the sheets. At this point they were exhausted and decided to break for food. They had a quiet meal together. Rob asked questions every now and then but the tension in the room was palpable.

The next couple days pretty much went the same way. Once the POD was delivered, they were able to take the furniture apart and pack it into the POD. Securing the container until they could schedule for pick up. The last night, the apartment empty and everything stowed away in either their bags or the POD, they decided to get a hotel room. They got one room with two beds. Steven and Ericka crashed on one while Rob took the other. Ericka drifted off to sleep quickly, but Steven just watched her. He heard a chuckle from Rob's bed and looked up to find him watching Steven.

"Was this what you were going to talk to me about when you picked us up in the car?" Rob asked.

Nodding Steven said, "I didn't know if I should cross that line of friend and family and wanted to know when you knew for sure to cross that friend line."

Softly laughing Rob said, "I was very stubborn. Believe me, that did not stop our flirting and things," he coughed and kept going, "But I didn't really admit to myself that I was in love with her until months after the flirting began. I don't think you have anything to worry about though. I have seen the way you look at her and the way she looks at you and it's the same way I look at Jemma." Picking up his phone he added, "Although your timing is horrible. The poor girl is a wreck. Just promise me you'll keep her close." Steven nodded.

The next morning, they met the POD container pick up crew and verified delivery address and they hauled it away. Ericka had to do her move out stuff with the apartment complex so she and Steven stayed there at the apartment as Rob worked via his phone and laptop on some business at the Starbucks around the corner. They weren't sure what they were going to do with Ericka's car and at the last moment she decided to sell it. So, Ericka sold it to Rob and then after Rob finished his business, he drove the car down to a dealer and sold it and took a taxi back. They were just leaving the apartment office when the taxi pulled up. Rob got out and had a frown on his face. "Have you been in there the whole time?" he asked.

Steven said, "Yes, why?"

Rob said, "Let's grab our things quickly. I saw an empty beat-up brown truck in the parking lot as I pulled in."

Grabbing their things, they piled back into the taxi, who had waited for them, and they went to the airport. They were a little early for their flight but that was ok. They were away from the brown truck. Looking over at Ericka, Steven could tell she was sad. He didn't know what he could do to make her feel better. He just held and stroked her hand and when she needed it, he would hug her.

"Do you think he'll follow me to the island Steven?" She whispered into his chest.

"I don't know. He does seem to be persistent that's for sure. I wonder how he found you in the first place." He asked.

Sitting up Ericka looked at Steven and Rob. "I think we are doing this wrong." They both turned and looked at her.

"What do you mean?" Rob asked.

"I think he will expect me to go to the island since my best friend is there. He probably already has a ticket." She stood and started pacing back and forth. "Something isn't right. I don't think I'm supposed to go to the island." She sat down. "Remember Rob how you set a trap for O'Leary? I think we need to set a trap for Chad or at least give him a false trail to follow."

Rob was sitting on the edge of his seat nodding his head. "I would have to agree with you Ericka. But I don't know how to keep you safe and do that too. If you remember I was very much against the trap that we laid out, which didn't really work, I might add."

Steven grabbed Ericka's hands and looked her in the eyes. "What are you thinking? Do you have an idea?"

"Yes," she said. "I think it's time to go home."

"What home? You mean Oregon?" questioned Steven.

Rob shook his head. "No Steven, she means home, home." Rob looked at her and asked, "Do you think you can do it? It is going to dredge up a lifetime of memories."

"This has to stop. I cannot move on with my life if I am always looking over my shoulder or packing up and moving. This is no way to live and I've lived it longer than I probably should have. I just never had the family I have now to help me make this step." She turned to Steven. "As long as you are with me, we can do this. What do you say?"

Kissing her quickly he said, "Let's end this."

Rob called and talked to Jemma and his dad. They agreed that Rob should fly out to the island and keep an eye on things for a few days in case Chad shows up and then Rob and Mike, with body guard in tow, would fly out to meet Ericka and Steven. They agreed that Ericka and Steven would lay low for a few days in case Chad had informants that would alert him to Ericka's presence.

When it was time to board all three went to the line and at the last second, Steven and Ericka hid in the group that had just arrived and headed back to the ticket booth to get their new tickets.

Chapter 10

As Ericka and Steven were flying into O'Hare International Airport, Ericka's anxiety was at an all-time high. She hadn't been back here in years. She hadn't seen or spoke to her aunt and uncle since she was in New York. They knew Chad's history and were happy she was able to get out of that situation even though they missed her. Bouncing her knee, Ericka was looking out over the place she grew up. Steven placed his hand on her knee and lightly squeezed.

"Want to talk about it?" he asked.

Shaking her head, she said, "Let's get settled in the hotel before I spill all the boring details that was Annie Chandler's life."

"Do you have any family still in Lombard?" he asked.

Nodding she said, "My aunt and uncle still live-in town. I haven't seen them in years. They helped me so much after Chad got worse. They knew I needed to disappear and understood why I couldn't stay in touch." Sighing she said, "Doesn't make it any easier though. When you have to leave everything, you've ever known behind and start over with no one to support you or even talk to. I couldn't even call them except on rare occasions. We were all afraid he would trace any calls to them."

The fasten seat belt light came on and the pilot came on the speaker announcing their arrival at O'Hare and to prepare for landing. Ericka took Steven's hand and kissed it. "Thank you for being here with me."

Tucking a strand of hair behind her ear, Steven smiled. "There is no other place I'd rather be than with you. I am very proud of you and your courage to return knowing what is to come."

After landing and getting their baggage, they flagged down a taxi and decided to find a hotel close by for the night so they could plan what they needed to accomplish. After finding a room and ordering dinner they collapsed on the bed both of them drained from the past few days. Steven called Rob and Jemma to let them know they landed and to check on them. Having no news on their end they planned to get back in touch with each other in a few days' time. Rob was adamant that they go no longer than a couple days without checking in.

Holding each other in bed, Steven kissed the top of Ericka's head and asked, "Are you ready to tell me your story?"

"Yes. It's time. It's time to put an end to all of this so we can move forward." She looked up into his face. "I want to move forward with you Steven. I don't want to be scared all the time anymore."

"I don't want you to be scared either." Pulling her close, "Let's start at the beginning then, shall we?"

Taking a deep cleansing breath, she began her story. "I was born Anne Chandler, but everyone called me Annie. My parents were Mark and Connie Chandler. My parents were killed in a car accident when I was 4 and I went to live with my aunt and uncle, Sandra and Richard Chandler. They raised me as their own since they were never able to have children. They loved me like I was their own, which was great seeing as I don't have many memories of my parents. They are the only parents I have ever known. I was a typical kid and rebelled during my early high school years but straightened out like most kids do when it was time to start on their own. I was planning on moving to Chicago, getting a place of my own and taking classes and working. I had my whole life mapped out and I was happy." Taking a cleansing breath, she continued. "It was July after my Senior year when I met Chad. My friends and I decided to go to a local concert and that is where I met Chad and his buddies. We clicked right away and we started dating. By the time September rolled around all my plans got pushed aside. Looking back now I can see how he started controlling things from the beginning but being in what I thought was love and never having had a serious relationship before I didn't notice the signs. My aunt did though. She tried to warn me but I wouldn't listen. In October I moved in with him and I was working as a waitress at a local restaurant while he worked construction jobs. Not unlike your family." She smiled at Steven and snuggled closer. She couldn't get close enough to him.

"November came and we decided to get married even though my family was against it. We decided just a quick ceremony with all our friends and family. Funny now that I look back on it, most of the guests were his friends. I had one or two people plus my aunt and uncle. Even though they didn't agree, they still came and supported me.

Things were great for the first year. Then I noticed that he was having more late evenings with the guys from work but other than that there was no sign about what was to come. That next Christmas things changed. Chad was having a hard time at work and he was drinking more. I noticed he was keeping odd hours and his friends were staying at our place all the time. When I asked him if there was anything wrong, he back handed me. I collapsed and

151

was in shock. He had never raised a hand to me in the whole year we had been married and dating. He apologized of course saying he didn't know where that came from and he would never do it again. I was young and naïve and I believed him. Things continued down this path for about six months with the odd outburst here a backhand or shove there. Every time we would make up right away and have sex. His way of showing me how much he loved me. Or so he said. Soon it was more than just the small hits. He started to be forceful in bed, to the point that I had to seek medical attention at one point. It was at this point that I felt stuck. He was beating me so he could get aroused and have sex. Sometimes he forced himself on me even when I fought and tried to get away from him. Those times he would beat me after sex as a punishment for fighting him.

My dear friend Grace, who had gone through her own war with her ex-husband, ran into me at the store one time and we got to talking. Of course, I had bruises on my arms and face, so I hardly ever wore short sleeve shirts or tank tops so people wouldn't see. But the bruises on the face were harder to cover up. Make up can only do so much. Grace invited me to a support group where no one asked who you were but just offered support. I started attending and slowly gathered my courage to get away from Chad. The first thing we did was move me out and filed a restraining order. It's funny how people say just get a restraining order and he can't touch you. Oh, he walked right through that restraining order, and beat me and threatened me with more to come. That piece of paper didn't protect me one bit.

The first time he found me, he put me in the hospital. My aunt Sandra stayed with me and I told her I had left him but he still came and beat me. We decided then to start the process for divorce. I knew he wouldn't care but legally I wanted nothing to do with Chad. Two men from the support group served Chad with the papers and he lost it. One of the men ended up with a broken nose and they said that when they served him, they could see what looked like cocaine or meth on the table. Chad was arrested for assault and battery and served 30 days since he didn't have the money to pay the fine. During his time in jail, I moved again. I was still in Lombard but I was in a completely different part of town. But after he got out, he followed my aunt Sandra to my new place and then waited until she left to come for me again. Luckily, I saw him coming so I was able to hide and call 911. But he knew where I lived now.

He started following me everywhere and making my life hell. I talked to my aunt and since the divorce was final by this time she suggested a move to Chicago, close enough to them but big enough to get lost. But he found me again this time putting me in the ICU. It was during this hospital stay that Grace and my aunt suggested changing my name so it would be harder to find me. We started the process and that is when I moved to New York. I cut off all contact with my aunt and uncle and even though he harassed them for a while he never physically touched them. Grace knew where I was but Chad didn't know who Grace was.

I was safe in New York for almost two years. It was wonderful. But I got lazy and that's when he pounced. The rest of the story you know. That is the sad tale of a young and naïve girl who thought she knew what love was." Turning to look up at Steven, she said, "I'm scared about going into Lombard. He still has friends there that I'm sure will inform him the moment I set foot in town. But I would love to see my aunt and uncle. It has been so long."

"Well," Steven said, "Why don't I reach out to them. Chad's friends don't know who I am and I could arrange for your aunt and uncle to meet you some place safe until we decided how we want to proceed."

Smiling she said, "I was kind of hoping you would offer. I really think that's the only way right now. I have changed in the years since I was the scrawny bean pole of a girl but my face really hasn't changed."

Rubbing his hands up and down her back and arm he said, "You are definitely not scrawny now, in fact I would say you are certainly curvy in all the right places." This time instead of going back up her arm, he trailed his hand down to her bottom and cupped her butt cheek sending an electric current through Ericka's body.

She started tracing his ribs and her wandering hands mapped out Steven's chest and thigh. Squeezing his thigh she brushed her hand along the bulge in his pants, just ever so slightly on her way back up his chest and up his neck to the back of his neck forcing him to lower his head so she could kiss him.

It started as a gentle and loving kiss, but it quickly escalated to a fiery and passionate kiss. Pulling back Steven smiled. "You've been killing me with the brushes up against my body. I don't want you to feel any pressure so if you don't want to be intimate that's fine, we will stop now."

He barely got the word 'now' out before she was on him straddling him with his face in her hands. She was kissing him tenderly but also rocking against him. He had tingles running throughout his entire body. He wanted to take his time and savor the moment but Ericka had other plans. She needed him now and with each rock against him she moaned.

Steven reached for her shirt bringing it up and over her head. He made short work of removing her bra and he had an up-close view of her fantastic breasts. Taking each breast in hand he massaged them while tormenting her nipples with his thumb and forefinger. Throwing her head back, she arched bringing those glorious globes within inches of his mouth. Sucking a nipple into his mouth he toyed with it. Her hands made their way to his hair and she held him in place. Encouraging him to move to the other breast, all the while still rocking against his bulge.

Impatient now she tried to get his shirt off so she could feel his skin. She wanted to rub her bare chest against his and feel the wiry hair from his chest against her sensitive nipples. Releasing her breast, Steven pulled her face toward him for a deep and sensual kiss. Leaning back, he pulled his shirt off and undid her pants while she fumbled with his. "You realize you will need to get off me in order to take off your clothes." He said playfully.

Smacking his shoulder, she rolled off him. He felt her loss immediately. They both removed the last of their clothes and stood there looking at each other from the other side of the bed. She couldn't stop looking at his erection, which was long and thick while also standing at attention. All she wanted to do was wrap her hand around him. Noticing her gaze, he stroked himself a couple times keeping her attention fixed on his hand. Watching Steven, Ericka climbed onto the bed and crawled toward him. Stroking himself faster, his eyes never left hers as she sensually crawled across the bed until she was kneeling in front of him. She placed on hand on his cheek while entwining her free hand with his that was around his erection, "Come, make love to me."

He looked down into her beautiful face and rested his forehead against hers. She pulled him into the bed and on top of her. Bracing himself he placed a hand on either side of her head on the bed and kissed her until she was breathless and panting his name. Kissing her jaw and then down her neck, he attacked her nipples once again. This time he wedged a knee between her legs making her open up to him. Pulling back, he took in the lovely picture she made laying there on the bed naked and spread open for him. She was breathtaking. He cupped her mound and slid a finger back and forth through her folds, making her groan with need. "You are so wet for me Ericka." Sliding one finger inside her she arched and moaned. Sliding a second finger into her core she bucked while trying to catch her breath. She groaned when he increased his pace. He pulled away and nudged her legs wide. He looked down and she tried to cover herself. "No, you don't. You are beautiful, every bit of you. He stroked his erection again while he looked at her. Soon she could feel the tip of him pressing against her entrance. She was not some scared young virgin, oh no, she knew what she liked and she was not afraid to share those things with Steven. He slowly pushed into her. She reached around him and squeezed his butt cheek.

With one long and deep thrust he was fully seated inside Ericka. Then he rolled back and thrust again. This time making Ericka moan. She hooked a leg behind him to encourage him to go deep. Looking up into Steven's eyes, the only thing she saw was the same hunger she felt for him. "I am yours Steven, only you." She whispered. A growl emanated from his chest and he thrust harder and faster. "Oh God yes, harder Steven."

She looked into his eyes as she came apart in his arms moaning his name. Steven felt her body clench around him and he thrust two more times while her muscles pulled him deeper than ever and he groaned as he pulled out and fell over the edge onto her stomach.

Collapsing on top of Ericka, it took a few minutes for him to catch his breath. He rolled off her and onto his back, taking her with him. He kissed the top of her head as she laid it on his chest. She was absentmindedly playing with hair on his chest, while he was rubbing her back. They laid in each other's arms and knew this was where they were supposed to be. As he drifted to sleep, he realized that he had never felt this sated in his life, nor felt this strong need to protect someone. He did though, and he knew he would gladly sacrifice himself to keep Ericka safe. Thinking back to the conversation with Rob, he remembered the question he asked, *'Are you willing to fight to keep that person in your life?'* Steven knew his answer; yes, yes, he would!

Chapter 11

Steven slowly woke the next morning to the feeling of a warm, curvy body pressed against him. He had a blanket of hair across his chest, her arm around his waist and a leg draped over his thigh. He had never felt this amazing first thing in the morning before. He looked down and saw she was still sleeping. She seemed so relaxed and content. He brushed her hair from her brow so he could see her face better. How anyone could ever physically and emotionally hurt this woman was beyond him. She had an inner strength that made her even more beautiful. And with all the crap she has had to deal with she was still such a caring and compassionate person.

Ericka had felt when Steven woke up. She laid there feeling his body under her and how he caressed her, brushing her hair out of her face. She was happy, too happy. She was afraid to open her eyes and have this be a dream. She heard Steven sigh and Ericka tightened her hold on his waist causing him to look down into her now open eyes. "I didn't want to open my eyes. I was afraid this was a dream and I didn't want it to end." She whispered into his chest.

He tightened his hold and said, "No dream. You are stuck with me. But I understand your fears. There is still so much uncertainty around us. Just know this," he pulled her up closer to his face and kissed her quickly, "This between us," he motioned back and forth between them. "This is certain."

She leaned into him and kissed him slow and languorously. Dragging her arm slowly up his chest, stopping by his flat nipple then continuing on to caress his cheek. Dragging him closer she deepened the kiss. His hands were busy massaging her back and bottom. She pulled herself up and straddled him, giving him access to her breasts. He grabbed a nipple with his mouth and the other with his hand while she scooted down and raised to her knees. Locking gazes, she slowly lowered herself onto him. Causing him to moan, "God you feel so good." He moaned.

He moved his hands to her hips and raised her up and brought her back down again, while he tilted his hips. Gasping Ericka smiled and threw her head back groaning, "Yes Steven."

She sped up the rhythm and he was lost in the awe watching Ericka ride him and taking her own pleasure. She was in the throes of passion and she was breathtaking. He met her, thrust for thrust, and groan for groan. They were perfect together and he had never felt this close to another human being. He felt her muscles start to clench around him but he was determined to last. He flipped her over onto her back and pounded into her thrust after thrust until she cried out her release. With one more thrust he withdrew and spilled himself on her stomach.

Rolling off of Ericka, he smiled, "That was some wake-up call. I could get used to that." And he kissed her temple bringing her back under his arm while trying to catch his breath.

She giggled and smacked his chest. "Stop it."

*   *   *   *   *   *   *   *

Looking up into his face she saw the love she felt reflected back to her. How did she get so lucky? One thing was for sure, she wasn't going to let anything or anyone come between them. She raised up and kissed him slowly. "I'm starving. Let's grab something to eat and figure out how to get my aunt and uncle to come to Chicago."

He rolled her back onto her back and kissed her. "What if I'm not ready to leave our bed?" He asked while nibbling on her neck.

Breathlessly she said, "Well I am open to negotiations. Do you have another idea?"

162

Taking her mouth with his, he proceeded to show her what his counter offer was.

An hour later, still wrapped in their bed sheets, there was a knock at the door. Steven grabbed his pants and quickly got their room service they had ordered. Ericka grabbed Steven's t shirt and threw it on. When he turned around his breath caught in his throat. He would always remember her in this moment. Wearing his t shirt, hair tousled and lips red from kissing, sitting cross legged on the bed looking up at him. He wasn't sure how they were going to get out of their room today. As he proceeded to set up a picnic on the bed, he thought maybe they didn't have to leave the room today.

Buttering her toast, Ericka turned to Steven, "Do you have a plan to contact my family?"

Steven swallowed his bite and said, "Well I was thinking about that. I think if I approach them as a friend of Grace, they might think I may be a friend of yours as well. What do you think?"

It was a good plan. Nodding she said, "That would probably work. We just need to figure out what to say and where to have them meet us."

They spent the rest of the morning coming up with a plan and figuring out what Steven would say to her aunt and uncle. It was after lunch when Steven called and aunt Sandra answered.

"Hello", she said.

"Hello, Mrs. Chandler. My name is Steven Morgan. My friend, Grace gave me your number. She said she met you at a hospital a few years ago. We have a mutual friend that would like me to see if you might be interested in meeting."

There was a gasp on the other end of the line. "Grace, you said." She shakily asked.

"Yes Ma'am. My friend is good friends with Grace." He responded.

"What exactly are you asking. Your friend wants to meet me?" She asked.

"Yes. You and your husband. She has recently come to Chicago and wanted to see if you could meet her." He replied.

"If this friend is who I think it is, there is nothing more I'd love to do. But I don't know if it's safe for her here" she said quietly.

"I know about the situation Ma'am. We were wondering if you might like to come to dinner here in Chicago while she is here. She would love to see you." He spoke.

"That would probably be best for now." She replied. They hashed out the details and said good bye.

Steven turned to Ericka who had been by the window listening to the conversation. She wiped a tear from her cheek and turned to him. "I haven't heard her voice in a couple years." Taking a deep breath, she walked to him and hugged him. "Thank you for doing this, Steven."

He held her in his arms, rubbing his hands up and down her back, whispering words of love into her ear. They spent a quiet evening at the hotel enjoying each other and trying to put everything else out of their minds.

As she was drifting off to sleep, wrapped in Steven's arms, she said, "I'm nervous about seeing them but excited. I just feel like I'm standing at the edge of something and I'm afraid of what that something is. I feel like there is something hovering at the edges and I can't quite make it out. No matter what happens though, please know how much I care for you Steven. I have always held back with making relationships because of the uncertainty of all this." She raised herself up on her elbows and kissed him. "I know I told you I love you at your parents' house. But I need you to understand it scares me. This is all new to me." He caressed her cheek. She turned into his palm, kissing it and said it again, "But I do love you, Steven. With a love that is both unfamiliar and familiar to me. The feelings are new to me but I feel like my soul has always known you. I am yours in every sense of the word and I needed you to know that before we step off the cliff and into the unknown."

Steven had sat up as soon as she had said the word love. How was he so lucky to have a woman like Ericka love him. He held her face in his hands and kissed her. "I love you, Ericka. I feel like my soul has been searching for you and didn't know it. I have been lost, wandering this earth alone. When I met you, I felt an instant connection and I know you felt that connection too. I think that is why we became such great friends. I think we were both a little leery to take the next step in our relationship because of our pasts. But I also believe that this is how it was supposed to play out. We were destined to be together, you and I. I feel that deep down in my bones." He wiped a tear off her cheek with his thumb.

"Steven, I," She couldn't finish the statement. She wrapped her arms around him and buried her face in his neck and cried. She was so happy but scared to lose the one thing that meant the most to her.

They fell asleep wrapped in each other's arms whispering words of love. What was going to happen next, they didn't know, but they both knew how much they loved each other and that would never change.

Chapter 12

Ericka was anxious waiting for the time to meet her aunt and uncle. Having extra energy, they decided to go for a walk. Ericka took Steven to the giant bean and they walked around the park to kill some time. It was just what she needed. After last night's pillow talk, Ericka felt a calming peace about Steven and knew this was the mate of her soul. Now if she could just get rid of the problem with Chad they could move on.

Finally, it was time to get ready and head to Morton's Steakhouse. They had decided on an early reservation so there could be less people. While out on their walk, Ericka had popped into a cute boutique and grabbed a new dress for the occasion. It was a cute summer dress with spaghetti straps. Steven looked handsome in his khakis and Polo shirt. She came out of the bathroom and Steven just stared. She had left her hair down and the dress fit her perfectly. She looked down and then back up at him. "Do you think it's ok?" She asked him nervous now.

"You look beautiful. I just don't remember you ever wearing your hair like that. I like it." He answered.

Blushing she gave him a quick kiss. "You are looking mighty handsome yourself sir."

He grabbed her around her waist and brought her to his chest. "Are you ready? It's ok to be nervous. Just know I won't leave your side." And he kissed her forehead.

Closing her eyes, she drank in his scent and savored the feel of his arms around her. She felt so safe in his arms. She knew this was going to go well. She was nervous but excited too. Looking up into his eyes she said, "Let's do this."

They made it to Morton's and decided to wait outside for her aunt and uncle, until their table was ready. Fidgeting Ericka, played with her hair and Steven knew she was nervous and excited. He took her hand in his and kissed it. She turned and over his shoulder she saw something. He turned to look at what it was and saw the older couple walking down the street. When Sandra caught sight of Ericka, she covered her mouth with her hands and turned to Richard and he wrapped his arm around her shoulder. Ericka rushed to them wrapping her arms around them. All three of them had tears streaming down their faces. Steven got choked up watching the reunion.

They finally made it back to where Steven was and he put his arm around Ericka. She turned to him and said,

169

"Steven, this is my aunt and uncle. Sandra and Richard Chandler." Turning to her aunt and uncle she said, "And this is Steven Morgan. My best friend and love of my life."

Steven reached out and shook Richard's hand and aunt Sandra hugged him whispering, "Thank you," in his ear.

Their table now ready they made their way into the restaurant. The three of them got caught up on what was going in Lombard. The store was doing great and this time of year with all the festivities they were busier than ever. "It can be tiring though. Long days standing or stocking all day really adds wear and tear to the old body." Uncle Richard laughed. "But we have been able to stay in competition with most stores. We are always looking for new ideas and ways to make the store better."

"We get to see a lot of friends being one of the main shoppes in the village," her aunt Sandra said. "It is always fun to see kids that we watched grow up come home and come visit the shop. Our old employees still stop by to check on the store and to say hi. We are even looking at creating an online presence, but that may come at a later time."

Ericka started to update them on what she had been up to. She told them about Chad finding her in New York. Her aunt Sandra took her hand and squeezed it. She explained how she got away and told them about Mary and

George Howard. She told them of the work that Mary and George did with domestic abuse victims. She let them know that she had stayed with them in Atlanta for a few days before making her way to Los Angeles.

"I was so inspired by Mary and George that when I enrolled at the college in LA and saw Jemma, Steven's sister, and the signs of abuse, I just had to reach out to her. At first, she was resistant, not wanting to make a bad situation worse. But eventually I was able to help her, but not before a couple hospital stays. It was at this time that I met Steven and the rest of the Morgan family. Steven and Grant, his older brother, had come down with their mom to try and get Jemma to leave Clint. It was then that I became an unofficial Morgan. Steven and I have been friends since we first met and it wasn't until recently that we realized what we were each searching for was each other." She finished and looked at Steven who picked up her other hand and kissed it.

Ericka shared that she had been taking classes at random until LA where she was able to finish and get her degree. "Steven and Jemma surprised me and came for my graduation. It was special but more so because I got to share it with my two best friends."

Ericka told them about Jemma and Rob's love story and kidnapping. "The Morgan family are no strangers to crazy people it would seem, between Clint, Rob's nemesis and now Chad. As much as I don't want to bring them into this, they do have a unique set of skills." Ericka joked.

Steven laughed and squeezed her knee. "I just recently learned about Chad and Ericka's story. When I flew in to LA my flight to Portland had been cancelled. So instead of staying at the airport I went to Ericka's. I knew that Jemma was going to be flying in to surprise her so I just tagged along." He picked up her hand and twined their fingers. "And I am so very glad that I did. It seems our timing has finally aligned."

Ericka said, "Well after dinner we can head over to our hotel and we can have a long chat about what's going on with Chad."

All through dinner Steven answered questions and he shared more about himself with Ericka's family. She had her hand on his knee and she would squeeze encouragingly every now and then. Steven explained he had a degree in business and after college had started up a dot com company, which he just recently sold and that he is on the lookout for another venture. He told Ericka's aunt and uncle that he has just been traveling and visiting friends and family while he searches for his next project. Steven told them that his dad, Trevor, owned his own construction company in Portland, Oregon.

He said that his older brother Grant was his partner and worked the family business which gave Steven the chance to explore. But he has on occasion worked in the construction field with his family. When tough times hit, they all pulled together and kept the business going. He was no stranger to hard work he told them. By the time dinner was over they were all ready to talk about the situation with Chad.

They walked to the hotel, deciding to sit in the lounge so they could all be comfortable. Ericka started the conversation, "Chad has found me again. When we were in Los Angeles, he was watching me and left a note for me in the middle of the night. We originally were going to fly back to Jemma's in Hawaii but I knew we were just putting off the inevitable. We have decided that it's time to face him once and for all so we," she said grabbing Steven's hand, "can move forward. We have not come up with a plan for once we are back in Lombard, but I wanted to see you and catch up before we head down that road."

"Well, we can tell you that he has a warrant out for his arrest. He has been dealing drugs and caused a lot of damage at one of the construction sites he was working at, so he ran. When he does come back all we have to do is call the cops." Turning to Richard he picked up her hand and her aunt continued, "He has been watching our house for quite a while. But before he ran, he confronted me about where you were. I honestly didn't know where you were after New York and he didn't like that answer." She looked down at her hands.

"Did he hurt you aunt?" Ericka asked.

"Not much but yes he did. He scared me more than anything. He is insane Ericka. He kept referring to you as Annie and rambled about you." She answered.

Ericka got up and knelt in front of her aunt. Crying she said, "I never wanted you to get hurt. This was my mistake but I didn't know how to fix it."

Her aunt caressed her cheek. "You are not to blame honey. You have tried everything to fix it. He is just an unstable man who needs to be put away for his own safety and the safety of the public."

They decided that Steven and Ericka would stay with them in Lombard and that Ericka could help out with their store. It would give her something to do as well as make herself noticed. If anyone was still watching her aunt and uncles, they would be sure to inform Chad of her return.

Saying goodbye brought just as many tears as the reunion. But they would head to Lombard the next day. After her aunt and uncle left, they went up to their room and

174

held each other. They still needed to come up with a trap but letting him know she was home was the first step.

"Steven, I think we should talk about what we are going to do about Chad." Ericka said. Looking up into his face she continued, "I want to have some kind of idea what we will do so we are prepared if he shows up."

"What are your thoughts? You know him better than anyone." Steven asked.

"I thought I knew him, but Chad strung out this bad is foreign territory for me. I would have never thought he'd hurt my aunt. So that goes to show I'm just as blind as the rest of you." She snuggled closer. "I do know he will have lookouts around town. He has his own little group of friends that keep each other informed about what's going on. As soon as we are seen about town the word will get back to him. Perhaps that's all we should do." She said and sat up and leaned on her elbow. "We need to be seen around town together so word gets back to him that I've come home. That should draw him out. And once he is out in the open, we shouldn't have too much trouble getting the police to pick him up for his outstanding warrant."

"I am ok with that plan on two conditions. One, you are not to be out and about alone, either your uncle or I need to be with you. And two, you need to communicate with me what's going on in here." He put his hand over her heart. "If you are scared or you sense something amiss, you need to make sure you don't try and do anything on your own." He said and took her face in his hands and kissed her.

That night they made love as if it could be the last time. Neither of them knew what was going to happen once they made her presence known. They drifted to sleep knowing tomorrow could be the end of the life on the run and the beginning of their life together.

Chapter 13

They rented a car the next day and made their way to Lombard. It was the perfect time to visit under normal circumstances. It was festival season and there would be lots going on and even more business at the store. There were blossoms everywhere as they entered the village.

"Wow, this is a beautiful place. Is it always like this?" Steven asked.

"This time of year, is festival season as all the lilacs and tulips are blooming. They have something each day or night for 16 days ending with the lilac parade. It's a really fun time of year around here normally." She answered. "I forgot just how beautiful this place is. There is a large park with all kinds of flowers. It really is a special place." She said turning to look at Steven.

Pulling up to her aunt and uncles house she sat there for a few minutes gathering herself. Her aunt opened the door and her uncle came out and helped Steven with their bags. Slowly Ericka got out of the car and looked at the house. Memories flooded her. It felt like the memories were from someone else. So much had happened between then and now. She was not the same person. Her aunt walked down the path to her and put her arm around her waist. Looking at her aunt she smiled and allowed her to guide her into the house.

Shutting the door, she saw Uncle Richard showing Steven around the house. She walked up the stairs to her room and opened the door. It was like a blast from the past. Everything was the same as she had left it. Touching the comforter as she passed by, she walked to the window. She knew nothing would ever be the same as this time capsule of a room. Looking out the window she saw a silver car parked down the street in front of a vacant lot. Well, if they were Chad's look out, he would soon get the message. She was home and she wasn't running.

That evening they ate out back and did some more catching up on things there in Lombard and Ericka's life in LA. After dessert they were just enjoying the evening when Uncle Richard asked. "Do you have a plan to get Chad here?"

Steven took her hand and she said, "I think me being out with Steven at the festivities would be the best way to draw him out. If he is as unstable as you say, people seeing us together and telling him we are a couple, that would be just what we need to draw him out."

Steven said, "I agree we need something to draw him out otherwise he is liable to just keep following you and watching from the shadows."

Richard said, "Well the Lilac ball is this weekend. We can definitely cause a stir there if you both want to come to it."

Ericka smiled. She couldn't remember the last time she had been to a dance. Other than dancing at Jemma's wedding, that is. Nodding she said, "I agree. That would be a great public place to be seen at."

They all said good night and Ericka giggled when Steven went into the room across from hers. "Best you remember what those giggles do to me." He whispered from across the hall. "Good night love. I am right here if you need me." Giving her a wink, he turned and walked into his room.

Ericka was still walking down memory-lane an hour later. Everything felt like time had just rewound and she was back in high school. Finally, she fell asleep around midnight. *She was at the park and the trees were in full bloom. Looking around she saw old friends from high school. They were all gathered for the festival picnic on Mother's Day. People were laughing and joking with her friends and aunt Sandra and uncle Richard like old times. There was a stage set up for the talent show. Jemma was there playing the piano. Which was odd since she didn't know Jemma back then. When the MC turned into Steven, Ericka knew her past and present were colliding in her dream. She tried to stand so she could go to Jemma and Steven but she couldn't get up from the bench. Everyone was still laughing and having a great time. Kids were running around blowing bubbles and sneaking cookies from the tables. She turned to say something to her uncle and it wasn't her uncle it was Chad. She tried to pull away from him but he had a hold of her wrists. Struggling against him, she turned to her friends who just turned the other way. She looked up at Steven and he was trying to get to her. Chad hit her across the face and she cried out. She started yelling Steven's name as he was blocked by some of Chad's friends. Chad stood up and drug her from the bench. Pulling her behind him, Chad just laughed while Ericka was yelling Steven's name. Chad started shaking her, "Ericka, stop." When she turned to look at him it wasn't Chad it was Steven. He shook her again. "Ericka love, wake up. It's ok I'm here." Steven wrapped his arms around her and she opened her eyes.*

Steven was in her room and had his arms around her. She was in bed with tears running down her face. Looking up she saw her aunt and uncle in the doorway. Aunt Sandra silently crying. She sat up and buried her face in Steven's

180

neck. "Shhh, you're ok. I'm here. Nothing can touch you here. You're safe." Steven was rubbing her back and talking into her hair. She wrapped her arms around him and whispered, "Please don't leave me Steven."

"Never. You are stuck with me love. You best get used to that." He answered quietly.

He turned to Ericka's aunt and uncle. "I hope you won't mind, but I'm not leaving her alone tonight." They nodded and left to go back to their room.

Getting into her bed, he pulled her to him and said, "Here on out, we stay together. No matter if we are awake or sleeping. Agreed?"

"100% agree." She responded. She snuggled closer she said, "Sorry about waking you up."

"I am not surprised you had a nightmare. This is a lot for your mind to take in. It has stirred up all your memories, the good and the bad. I am just glad that I'm here with you." He said and kissed the top of her head.

"Me, too." She tipped her head back and said, "I could use a good kiss to wipe those bad memories away. Know any one I could get one from?"

Pinching her bottom, playfully, he said, "I might know a guy."

And he kissed her. And oh, what a kiss. With Steven's arms around her and that kiss on her mind she was able to fall asleep peacefully for the rest of the night.

The next day, they all went down to the store to show Steven around. Uncle Richard was working so Ericka and Sandra gave Steven the tour of Lombard. Ericka showed him her old high school, the restaurant she used to work at and the park. They didn't get a chance to go exploring however, Richard called Sandra saying they were swamped and asked them to come help. This time of year, there are lots of tourists and families visiting.

On the way to the store they ran into Ricky Tucker, one of Chad's best friends. Ericka placed her arm around Steven who tightened his grip. He stopped them in their tracks, "Annie Chandler, well aren't you a sight for sore eyes. The years have been kind to you darlin'. Where is Chad? Oh, that's right you divorced him didn't you. I guess that explains why you are hanging on this fella."

"Ricky. I have no idea where Chad is. We've been divorced for years. If you'll excuse us, we are late." She said pulling Steven behind her.

"I don't like how he talked to you," Steven hissed. "Who was that?"

"That my love was Chad's best friend. If we wanted him to know I was in town, running into him will surely get that done." She replied.

"Well, you aren't to go anywhere without someone with you, ok? Promise me Ericka." He stopped her and turned her around to face him.

Cupping his face, she promised and kissed him for all to see.

At the store, they found uncle Richard busy with customers. Steven went into the back to get out of the way. And sat there thinking about the confrontation with Ricky. He didn't seem surprised to see her, and he was overly familiar with her. And the look he gave her was more of a leer. He didn't have a good feeling about this guy. While waiting he decided to call and check in with Rob.

"Hey we are in Lombard now, staying at Ericka's aunt and uncle's home. Any sighting of Chad there?" He asked Rob.

"It's all quiet here. How did the reunion go? Good I'm guessing since you are at their place." Rob asked.

"Their reunion was much needed by all of them, although coming here has dredged up a bunch of memories. She had a horrible nightmare last night." He confided. "And we just ran into Chad's best friend. I have a funny feeling, Rob. He looked at her like a piece of meat and was overly familiar. Almost like he was biding his time for his turn with her. Does that even make sense?" he whispered into the phone.

"Yes. You don't know what Chad has been telling people. You need to be alert and not let her out of your sight. Do you want me to fly out there? I can be there in a day or so." He asked.

Shaking his head Steven said, "I don't think we are there yet. Besides her uncle is a very capable man. I am sure between the two of us we can keep the women safe. I will keep you posted though. If you don't hear back from me in a couple days, plan on coming out, ok?"

Rob agreed and they hung up. Steven walked out to the store and watched as Ericka worked with her family, greeting old friends. Steven watched Ericka as she helped people in the store. Her entire face lit up. Seeing old friends and laughing with them made her even more beautiful. She worked behind the counter and was a natural. He realized that she had at one point worked there with her family.

184

*   *   *   *   *   *   *   *

Ericka caught Steven watching her a few times. Smiling at him she went about her various jobs and helped those who needed it. It was wonderful to be back behind the counter and seeing so many people she knew and missed. She walked over to Steven and introduced him to a couple ladies, who went to school with her. They called her Annie which made sense, as that is who she was during her high school days. That was going to take some getting used too.

They spent the rest of the day there at the store and Steven helped with restocking or fetching things here and there. It was rather nice being busy and not dwelling on Chad and now Ricky. She didn't trust Ricky either. He seemed more than capable of grabbing her for Chad.

Everyone was exhausted that evening. Steven and Ericka sat out back on the swing just watching the stars and enjoying the weather and being in each other's company. Looking down into Ericka's face, Steven asked, "After all this is over have you thought about what you want to do?"

She shook her head, "I have been living from moment to moment for so long I'm not sure what to do. Before you showed up on my doorstep in LA, I was just concentrating on finishing school. Now that's done I'm not sure what I am

185

going to do. What about you? You sold your company, now what are you going to do?" She asked.

"That is an excellent question. Before I landed on your doorstep, I was floundering, not really sure what I wanted to do. I like the fact that we are in the same head space. We can figure it out together." He kissed the end of her nose, making her giggle. "Ugh, you know what your giggles do to me lady." And he nuzzled and nibbled her neck causing her to giggle even more. "Lucky for you, your aunt and uncle are here."

They laughed and turned their attention back to the stars. It was a beautiful night.

The next day Ericka decided to take Steven to the park and go for picnic. They enjoyed seeing all the festivities and all the beautiful blossoms. The entire park was decked out with all kinds of tulips and lilacs. The gazebo there in the park seemed to the center for all the festivities. They didn't even need to pack a lunch as there were so many booths and vendors set up around the outskirts of the park, they were able to get lunch there. They ran into more of Ericka's or rather Annie's old classmates. They all seemed genuinely happy to see her. Ericka never really mentioned friends, except that she didn't have many after Chad was in the picture. She really hoped that without Chad she would be able to rekindle some of those friendships.

They were on their way out of the park when they spotted Ricky again, this time he wasn't alone. He didn't approach them but he watched them. Steven pulled Ericka closer and they continued on to the Chandler's house. Steven didn't have a good feeling about that guy. Something told him that he was just as big a threat as Chad.

*   *   *   *   *   *   *   *

The time flew by with an occasional sighting of friends and Ricky. Soon it was time to plan for the ball. Ericka decided she needed a new dress so Sandra and Ericka went shopping with Steven there for protection. The ladies were inside trying on dresses while Steven waited out front. Sitting on a bench outside the store, Steven relaxed and took in the village and its many residents. He watched as a mother and toddler crossed the street to go to the park, which conjured an image of Ericka pregnant with their child. She would be a great mom. But were they to that point yet? No. Until all the uncertainty of Chad was resolved they couldn't plan that far ahead. However, he could plan something else. Just as he was formulating a plan, Ericka and Sandra came out of the store laughing and smiling. It was so good to see her looking so happy.

"Well ladies, did you buy the store out or did you save some for others?" he teased.

Ericka playfully smacked his shoulder, "Very funny sir. But a lady must look good so she might be able to have fellas want to dance with her you know."

Growling low in his throat he whispered in her ear, "There better be only one fellow on that list, my dear." And kissed her cheek.

Giggling and driving him crazy she said, "We will have to see."

She took his arm and pulled him along to the store where Richard was working. They were all going to grab lunch together before heading back to the house. As they walked into the restaurant, Steven took Richard aside, "I would like to have a chat with you later if you have time."

Smiling, Richard put his hand on Steven's shoulder and said, "Of course. After dinner tonight we will have a little chat."

As they rejoined the ladies, Ericka turned to Steven with a raised eyebrow, "What was that about?" she asked.

"Oh nothing. I thought we could have a chat and I could get some fun stories from your uncle about you." He replied.

Eyebrows still raised she turned her attention to her aunt who was asking her a question about the menu. Steven sat down and looked at Ericka huddled with her aunt. He was glad that they were able to reunite. He knew how lonely Ericka had been because he had been too, even though he had his family around. It was like he was searching for Ericka, even though he hadn't realized it.

They had a great visit but lunch went quickly. Soon Richard needed to head back to the store with Sandra. This gave Ericka and Steven, some much needed, quiet time. They still needed to come up with a plan about Chad. They decided to walk home leaving the car with her aunt for later. Walking hand in hand Steven asked questions about her life growing up in the Village. Where her favorite places were in town and what she did with her friends. Pulling him toward the park, Ericka showed him one of her favorite places. She told him of the times she would sneak out and just come here to think or get away from her life.

They sat under a huge maple tree and watched the activity around them. The park was a bustling hive of activity right now. Leaning back against the trunk of the tree,

Ericka closed her eyes and said, "This used to be my spot. I would come here even during the winter to get away. Lean back Steven, and close your eyes. Take a deep breath and smell the amazing flowers."

He did as she said and leaned against the tree and closed his eyes. He reached out and took her hand, rubbing it with his thumb. "Thank you for sharing this with me." He cracked one eye to look at her. She was smiling with her eyes closed and she was the most beautiful thing he had ever seen. "But to be honest I have seen something more beautiful than this park."

She turned to look at him and said, "Really?!"

Nodding he leaned in and kissed her. "Yes, really and I'm sitting right next to it."

She shoved her shoulder into his and said, "Oh stop. I do not compare to these beautiful blooms. But I thank you for the compliment anyway. A lady does love to be compared to flowers."

He reached out and wrapped his arms around her and she snuggled into his chest. "Even with all the people right now, this is such a peaceful place. I can always calm my mind and reset my thinking when I come to visit here."

He leaned in and kissed the top of her head and said, "I have to say I am glad that you have been able to come home and reconnect with your family. It is super important since it's such a big part of who you are."

"I am too." She whispered. Standing she pulled him up. "Thank you for being here with me." She wrapped her arms around his waist and laid her head on his chest. He wrapped his arms around her, pulled her closer and kissed her temple. "Ok," she pulled back from him and grabbed his hands. Pulling him behind her, she made her way to the path. "Let's walk around. I want to see all the exhibits and craft booths."

They walked around the park, stopping here and there to see what was displayed. Ericka found a gorgeous necklace and earring set, from a local silver craftsman, to go with her outfit for the ball. Steven found a bracelet for his mom for Mother's Day. The afternoon passed by quickly and before they knew it, the sun was setting and they had to head to the house. Steven was anxious to have his chat with Richard after dinner.

While Ericka was showing Sandra the items, she had found at the craft fair, Richard and Steven went out back. Richard sat down on the bench and watched Steven as he paced back and forth on the porch. "Ok son, I have a feeling I know what you want to chat about. Why don't you just come out with it. You will feel better once you've uttered the words." He chuckled at him.

"I would like to ask for your permission to marry Ericka. We haven't talked about marriage yet, but I am planning a surprise proposal and I would like your blessing." He blurted.

Chuckling, Richard said, "Well you don't need my blessing, but you have it all the same. I see how you both look at each other. She has had a rough time of it with Chad but I know you wouldn't ever hurt her, at least not on purpose anyway. I just ask two things from you. Please don't lose contact with us. I haven't seen Sandra this happy in years. She has her girl back and I am afraid of what losing her again would do to her. And second, will you consider using a family ring for the proposal. Ericka is the last of the Chandlers and I would love her to have my mother's ring." He stood and walked over to Steven, placed his hand on his shoulder and reached out with his other to shake his hand. "Please take care of my baby girl."

Steven's throat tightened with emotion. He nodded and said, "You have my word and I would be honored to use your mother's ring. I am sure Ericka would be overjoyed to have it as well."

Richard smacked him on the back and said, "Great. Now tell me, what is your plan for the proposal?"

They both sat down and Steven spent the rest of the evening laying out his plans with suggestions here and there from Richard. He couldn't wait to put his plan into motion, now that he had the family's approval and help, he knew, it would be a moment to remember for the rest of their lives.

Chapter 14

Ericka was starting to get a little worried. Steven had been acting weird all morning. The ball was tonight and she was worried that Steven might be having second thoughts about them. She wouldn't blame him really. She came with a lot of baggage and he was seeing most of it first-hand. Ericka was also wary as no one had seen Chad in weeks. Perhaps she had jumped to conclusions. But the cut harness and those flowers at her apartment had been evidence she wasn't dreaming this up. She needed to have a show down and get this chapter of her life finished so she could move on with Steven.

Steven left a little before lunch saying he needed to get his clothes for the ball tonight. Ericka thought that was an excuse to get out of the house though. Uncle Richard was at the store and aunt Sandra was home working around the house. Ericka decided to have a soak in the tub to try and relax. She really wasn't nervous about the ball but more of the unknown. Living under such constant uncertainty was wearing her down. Slipping into the tub, Ericka thought back to the last time she had been in this tub. It was right before she and Chad had moved in together. Aunt Sandra and Uncle Richard were upset with Ericka and they had just had a big fight. It is amazing how smells, places and people trigger memories. Here she was trying to move on from Chad and if she had just listened all those years ago, she wouldn't be in this position now. She needed to tell her aunt and uncle sorry for the heartache and worry she caused them.

Ericka closed her eyes and let the warm water relax her. She needed to gather her inner strength if she was going to meet this new trial head on. She owed it to herself, to her family and now to Steven. He deserved so much better than her, but she was selfish enough not to let him go. Her biggest fear, during all this, was Steven getting hurt or leaving. She knew it was a possibility as Chad was completely unstable. Who knew what he would do once Chad saw them as a couple? She should make him leave. If anything happened to him, she would never forgive herself. She doubted he would leave even if she begged. Taking a deep breath, she decided to make it through the ball and then talk to him about leaving. She knew it would be a battle but she couldn't put him in harm's way. Chad had already hurt her aunt. There was no way she was going to let anyone else get hurt because of her.

*   *   *   *   *   *   *   *

While Ericka was soaking in the tub, Steven was on his own mission, although had he known she would be in the tub he might not have been able to leave so easily. It was a good thing he left earlier that morning. Steven had gotten advice from Richard and was on a mission to make tonight extra special. He had decided he didn't want to propose in front of the town. He wanted something intimate and just for them. So timing was everything. Thank goodness he had Richards help so he could make sure Ericka stayed on time. Luckily the park was in full bloom so Steven really didn't need flowers, however he wanted to propose at sunset. It would be early enough there wouldn't be a lot of people there for the ball yet. The trick was trying to figure out how to get her there without giving it away. Talking it over with Richard they decided he would take her there before she got ready for a quiet picnic dinner. Richard would bring Ericka, blind folded so Steven only needed to set up the picnic and grab the dinner.

Steven dropped off the ring Richard asked him to use at the jewelers to get cleaned up and put into a special box. He also shopped that morning for clothes for the ball. He was trying to stay away from the house as long as possible. He was afraid he wouldn't wait and just blurt everything out. It was afternoon before Steven showed back up at the Chandler's house. Ericka had just gotten out of the tub and was in her robe. She was tempting to say the least. He decided he better take his shower so he could leave as soon as

196

possible. Taking his time, he tried to relax, but tonight was a big deal in more ways than one. If all went to plan, he would be engaged by this time tomorrow. Not to mention there was always the chance that Chad might make his appearance. That was a fear Steven had about the proposal. What if he tried to stop it or used it to try and hurt Ericka? All day long he kept second guessing himself. Should he wait or should he move forward? In the end he decided that he wouldn't let Chad dictate their lives any longer, so forward he went. Done with his shower, he shaved while trying to come up with an excuse to leave. What would she think? He had been gone all day long and now he bails? He hoped she was going to be forgiving once she saw what he had planned.

After his shower he called Richard to make sure everything was still a green light. Then he needed to go and get the ring and set up at the park. Thankfully Richard said it was a go and he would be home soon to distract Ericka. Steven went in search of Ericka to check in. Tonight, was a big deal for her and he wanted to make sure she was doing ok. He found her in their room wrapped up in a robe sitting in the window, looking outside. Walking into the room she turned and smiled at him. "Hey stranger. Did you get your errands all taken care of?" she asked, while standing up from the window.

"I did. I do have to run and get my suit though, there were some alterations they needed to make so it would be perfect. I just wanted to check on you and see how you were holding up." He said rubbing her arms.

"I'm as good as can be expected, I guess. So much unknown makes it hard to plan or think too far into the future. I wanted to check on you though. I'm worried for you Steven. Maybe you should head to Jemma's." Steven stopped his hands and cupped her face. "Not that I want you to leave Steven, I'm just worried you will be in the cross fire and I would never forgive myself if you got hurt."

Shaking his head, Steven said, "I am not going anywhere. Where ever you go I go! That has not changed just because it might get a little uncomfortable."

"Steven, it could be dangerous, not just uncomfortable. I'll tell you now, I'm scared. But also, I am tired. Tired of it all. I don't want to keep looking over my shoulder, but that doesn't mean you have to be in the middle of it." She turned and tried to walk back to the window.

"Oh no you don't. We are going to talk this out my dear. What has brought this on?" he asked.

"Well, I knew this might be dangerous the whole time, but hearing my aunt tell me that Chad hurt her, made me second guess bringing you, or any of the Morgan's and Harrington's into this crazy situation." She replied.

Wrapping his arms around her, he said, "I do believe Rob and I told you there was no getting rid of us. We take care of our family, and you are family Ericka." He kissed her slowly until she relaxed in his arms. Pulling back, he looked her in the eyes and said, "I'm not going anywhere, ok?"

"Ok." Ericka nodded and kissed him. "Don't you need to go get your suit?"

"I do but I might see if they can bring it." He replied.

Steven knew he couldn't leave Ericka. They were going to have to change his plans a bit. Hugging Ericka he said, "Let me make a couple calls, that way I won't have to leave. Maybe we could go for a walk before dinner and the ball."

Ericka nodded and said, "That sounds perfect. Thank you for thinking of me. I know I'm a bit demanding with all my baggage. I want you to know just how much I appreciate you." She wrapped her arms around his waist and slowly down to his bottom, giving him a playful squeeze.

"Now don't go starting something we can't finish right now." He said laughing.

"Go make your calls, sir, while I change." She said, pushing him toward the door.

"Yes ma'am." He said while swatting her bottom.

Out back Steven called Richard. "We are going to need to make a few changes. And I'm hoping I can enlist yours and Sandra's help." He proceeded to tell Richard what he wanted to do and see if they could pull it off. Richard was positive they could get it done, he just needed to get Sandra to the store so she could help. They hung up and as Steven walked into the kitchen, Sandra's phone rang. She answered and then looked at Steven with a big smile. She nodded to him and so he went in search of Ericka.

"Did you get it all straightened out?" Ericka asked as he walked in.

"I did. Although I think your aunt will be grabbing my suit for me. She had to run to the store for Richard. I heard her talking on the phone before I came in." he lied.

"Oh, good so we have time then." Ericka said while grabbing Steven's hand.

Laughing at Ericka's antics he said, "Not enough time to accomplish what is on your mind my love. I want to love on you all night long not a quick 15 minutes while the house is empty."

They both laughed at that. Ericka finished getting dressed and putting on her shoes. She started to get up when Steven realized she was ready to go. He needed to stall just a little bit to give Richard and Sandra time. He pulled Ericka back onto the bed and under him. "Who said we couldn't at least have a little fun though."

Kissing Ericka long and slow he proceeded to get them both worked up. Perhaps he should have chosen a different distraction. He might not make it to the tree for the proposal. Pulling back from her, Steven knew he needed to stop otherwise they wouldn't leave the room. Kissing her nose he said, "So is there a story behind everyone calling you Annie or is it just a nickname?"

Laughing at him, she said, "Well the original artist of the cartoon used to live here and I think everyone just associated me with little orphan Annie since my parent's passed away."

"Oh Ericka, I'm sorry I didn't mean to bring up a painful memory." He apologized.

"It's ok really. It doesn't make me sad. I know my parents loved me and I know what happened to them so I have the closure I needed. Growing up my aunt and uncle were mom and dad so I never really felt I had gone without." She said and kissed him. They sat there and just held each other, each thinking of how life changes, sometimes for the worse but also sometimes for the better.

"Ok, now that I've ruined the moment, are you ready for a walk?" he asked.

"Now would be perfect. That would give us enough time to walk, then come back and eat before heading to the ball. Besides it's almost sunset and the park is so beautiful right now. Let's go." She stood and pulled him up from the bed.

Walking hand in hand, they left the house and walked toward the park. It was really a beautiful day. Exactly how he hoped it would be. He just hoped that he had given Richard and Sandra enough time to set up the picnic. Looking ahead to the spot by the tree, he noticed Richard was still working and turned to Ericka, "Let's check out that wine booth. Maybe we can grab a bottle for later."

He steered Ericka toward the vendor booth and they sampled a couple wines before they bought a bottle. It actually ended up being the perfect distraction. Looking over Ericka's shoulder he saw the place was ready. Grabbing the bottle and Ericka's hand he steered them toward her tree.

When Ericka realized where he was directing her, she saw there was a picnic set up. She stopped, "Oh look someone else loves my spot too. It's so sweet. Let's leave whoever it is to their picnic." And she started to pull Steven away from her tree.

"What if I told you the picnic was for us?" he asked her.

Stunned she looked at him and he nodded at her. "I enlisted the help of your aunt and uncle to pull this surprise off."

He took her to the blanket and before she sat down, he bent on his knee and looked up at Ericka. "I love you, Ericka. I feel like my soul is finally at peace when I am with you. We have been friends longer than lovers but there is no other way I would have done this. To be able to ask your best friend to stay with you always, to love them and laugh with them and grow old with them is more than I deserve, but it is what I want. You are who I have been waiting for and I know you feel the same. I know this is a time of uncertainty but that makes this even more important to do this now. Ericka, or should I say Annie? I didn't think that part through." He said more to himself than anyone. Ericka laughed through the tears and he continued. "I want to start a life with you Ericka. No matter where you go, I want to be there as a friend, as a lover, and as a protector. Will you do me the honor of becoming my wife?"

Laughing and wiping her face, Ericka said, "Yes, please. I would love to marry you. I love you, Steven."

He stood and even though he wanted it to just be them, they had drawn a small crowd of onlookers who clapped and cheered as he placed the ring on her finger and kissed her. Ericka looked down at the ring and gasped. "Your uncle asked me to use this ring when I asked for permission to marry you. He said it was his mom's ring and that you were the last of the Chandlers. I hope you like it."

"I used to look at this ring all the time. I would go into aunt Sandra's closet and play dress up and this was my wedding ring. I am so happy it is where it was always meant to be. Thank you, Steven." She said and wrapped her arms around him and kissed him deeply.

The clearing of a throat brought them back to their surroundings. Looking up they saw Richard and Sandra standing there amongst the onlookers. Sandra was crying and Richard was smiling from ear to ear. "I think someone wants to congratulate us." Steven said and pointed to her aunt and uncle. Pulling away from Steven, Ericka walked over to her aunt and uncle and the three of them embraced.

Steven stood there watching and looked around. He caught sight of Ricky off to the side of the crowd and moved closer to Ericka. Ricky was on the phone, probably with

Chad. Well, if they wanted his attention, they just got it. He shook Richard's hand and got a kiss on the cheek from Sandra. Steven placed his hand on the small of her back, he said, "We have an audience. Why don't we take this back to the tree and have dinner?"

Richard looked over at Ricky and said, "You two go enjoy your dinner. We will break up the crowd."

Steering Ericka to the picnic they sat down. Steven placed Ericka to face away from Ricky and he sat so he could keep an eye on him. The crowd dispersed after they sat down. They enjoyed the dinner, the bottle of wine they had bought and the amazing sunset. With some reluctance they decided it was time to head back to the house and to get ready for the ball. They agreed they had a lot to celebrate tonight.

Chapter 15

Ericka was both excited and terrified to go to the ball tonight. She was so happy after the amazing dinner and proposal from Steven. She didn't want anything to mess up this amazing day but she knew deep down that going to the ball was going to bring up lots of memories and potentially lots of drama. But like she told Steven, she was tired of running and always looking over her shoulder. So, with trepidation, she finished getting dressed and headed to find her aunt and uncle. They would be attending the ball altogether.

Coming downstairs, she found Steven waiting at the bottom step for her with her aunt and uncle by the door. "You look amazing." Steven said. Taking both her hands in his he leaned in and kissed her.

"Thank you." She smiled at him. "You don't look half bad yourself. In fact, I better keep my eyes on you tonight." She teased. He pulled her closer laughing and squeezed her waist.

Laughing together they all left and walked to the park where the ball was being held. Taking a deep breath, she squeezed Steven's hand. "I'm a little nervous." She admitted.

"I would be worried if you weren't, love. Just know I am going to be with you every step of the way ok." He smiled at her then kissed the back of her hand.

As they got closer to the park Steven pulled Ericka closer. He wanted to make sure there was no doubt who was Ericka's partner tonight. He knew that Ricky would be there and was worried that Chad would use this ball as a distraction to try and grab Ericka. Richard had voiced his same concerns earlier that evening while they were waiting for the women to finish getting ready. They decided that no matter what happened Richard would keep an eye on both women and if there was trouble Richard was supposed to take both women home, immediately.

Walking into the area where the ball was being held, they saw lots of people. Ericka pointed out several people he had recently met and introduced him to several others. They were having a great time when the band started tuning their instruments. "Would you do me the honor of a dance, my love?" Steven asked.

"I would love too." She answered.

Taking his hand Ericka walked out onto the dance floor with several other couples. She really didn't know how to dance, but she just smiled. She would make the best out of this evening. Steven wrapped his arms around her and she did the same. She looked into his eyes and saw the love she felt reflected back at her. Ericka was happy. Happier than she had been in years. She leaned up and kissed Steven. "Thank you for being here Steven. I am truly a lucky lady to be engaged to such a kind and handsome man." She whispered.

Bending down he kissed her lips. "I am the lucky one Ericka. To have not only found my soul mate but to find my best friend and lover too is far more than I deserve."

Steven looked up and caught sight of Ricky off to the side of the dance floor. Pulling Ericka closer he whispered, "Ricky is here and he is watching us. No matter what happens tonight I want you to know how much I love you. Your uncle is keeping an eye on you tonight as well and we agreed, should anything happen, he will take you home with your aunt. Okay?"

Nodding she pulled Steven closer and said, "I love you too. Nothing will ever change that."

As the song ended, they held each other for a moment longer and slowly walked off the dance floor. Ericka felt the tension running through Steven. She knew he was worried but also wanted to confront Chad so they could be finished with him. Reaching her aunt and uncle they visited with friends who had gathered. The proposal earlier in the day had already started spreading through town and they were getting several congratulations from people. Slowly they all started to relax realizing there wasn't much concern with so many people around. Ericka just needed to make sure she didn't go anywhere alone. They watched Ricky throughout the evening but surprisingly there was no sign of Chad.

It was almost time to head home when Steven realized that Ricky had disappeared from the ball. He told Richard he was going to the restroom to see if he might be there. He didn't trust Ricky and felt he was just a bit too familiar with Ericka. On his way to the restrooms, he heard footsteps behind him. Slowing down he turned just as someone swung something at Steven's head. He felt a blinding pain and then his world went black.

Steven had been gone close to fifteen minutes, which was about ten minutes too long. Ericka looked at her uncle and saw he was worried too. "I promised I would get you both home safe, Ericka. Please come home with me and then I'll get some help and look for him, but only after I know you and your aunt are safe." Her uncle whispered.

"I don't want to leave without him." She kept searching the crowd of people. "Why can't we all just walk by the restrooms then go home?" she begged.

"Because I gave my word if I felt there was a problem, I would get you home. The longer we argue the longer it will be until I can look for him. Let's go now so I can come back while people are still here and can help." Ericka nodded.

She agreed it would be better if her uncle had people with him while looking for Steven. She hurried home with her aunt and uncle. Making promises to her uncle to stay put inside with all the doors and windows locked tight. Ericka was getting more worried with each minute passing and still no sight of Steven.

They arrived at the house and locked up. Running upstairs, Ericka changed. She wanted to be ready should they come back and Steven needed help. She needed to be prepared. She was worried that he might have gotten jumped by Ricky and his cronies. The longer her uncle was gone the more she worried. Giving up sitting down she started pacing the living room. She needed a distraction. Grabbing her phone, she decided to call Jemma.

"Hello," Jemma answered.

"Hey Jemma. It's Ericka." She said into the phone.

"Is everything ok?" Jemma asked.

"No. We were at the ball and having a wonderful evening, especially after Steven proposed, but Steven went to the restroom and never came back. My uncle gathered some neighbors and they are out searching for him." Ericka rambled. She was talking so fast she wasn't sure even Jemma could keep up with her.

"Wait, Steven proposed? But now he is missing?" Jemma asked. "Hang on Rob wants me to put you on speaker so we all can hear what's going on. Ok go ahead and tell us what's going on."

"Ok I was going to ask to talk to Rob anyway. I think Steven has already checked in with him about Ricky, Chad's friend. But I am so worried. Ricky has been following us around since we got to town. And he was there at the ball tonight but then toward the end we couldn't find him. Steven was worried he might be setting a trap for me for on the way home so he went to the restroom to see if he was in there, but never came back."

"Yes, he did check in with me and told me about Ricky, Ericka." Rob responded. "Where are you now? Are you safe?" he asked.

211

"Yes, my uncle made me and my aunt come home and lock the house up. I guess he and Steven had come up with a plan in case something like this happened. He is now back out at the area where the ball was held and is searching with some of his friends. But he has been gone at least 30 minutes. I am starting to get nervous Rob." Ericka confided.

"Ok I'm glad you are safe. I want you to promise me you won't leave unless you are with someone and even then, I don't think you leaving until Chad is apprehended is a good idea. I am glad Steven and your uncle made a plan. You need to have faith that Steven is ok. I want you to call me as soon as your uncle gets back though so we can plan." He pleaded.

"Wait! Don't you dare hang up Rob." Jemma yelled. "I need to talk about this proposal."

"Oh, I missed that, Steven finally proposed? I am assuming congratulations are in order." Rob said.

"Yes, he proposed tonight before the ball, by my favorite place in the park. But I'll have you save the congratulations until my uncle brings him home." Ericka said.

Ericka was in the kitchen, when she heard the front door. "Hang on. I hear the door." Ericka said.

Running into the living room she saw her uncle and their neighbor Gary. "Rob my uncle and his neighbor are here but Steven is not." Turning to her uncle she said, "Where is he?"

Shaking his head, Ericka's uncle said, "We looked everywhere and couldn't find him. But Ericka you need to sit down." He pulled her to the couch.

"Why do I need to sit down?" She asked.

"We found traces of blood on the ground near the bathrooms." Her uncle said.

"No. You must be wrong." She replied shaking her head.

Her uncle tried to take her hands and she wouldn't let him. She stood and started toward the door. "No Ericka you can't go out there. We don't know what's going on." Her uncle wrapped an arm around her and pulled her back toward the couch.

"No, I have to find him. Let me go uncle. I need to find Steven." She cried.

"Ericka." She heard, from a tunnel and realized she must have dropped the phone. Rob was yelling her name. "Ericka. Answer me." Rob yelled.

Picking up the phone, she said, "Rob did you hear what my uncle said? They found blood by the restrooms. I have to go look for him."

"No, you are going stay put and I'm going to fly in tomorrow and we will find him together." Rob said. "Promise me Ericka you will wait until I get there before you do anything."

Ericka was crying and buried her face in her uncle's chest. Uncle Richard said, "Rob, this is Richard Chandler, Ericka's uncle. I will make sure she stays put. We still have people at the park looking but most everyone has gone home from the ball. We could have missed them in the chaos of all the clean-up."

"My dad is booking our flights right now. When we hang up text me your address and we will be there as soon as possible." Rob responded.

"Ericka." Came a cry from the phone. "Please stay there until Rob and Mike can get to you. I don't want anything happening to you as well as to Steven. We will get through this and soon you will be planning your wedding." Sniffed Jemma.

"I never wanted him to get hurt. I knew coming here was a risk for me but I didn't think he would go after Steven, Jemma. I'm so sorry." Cried Ericka.

"This is not your fault Ericka. This is Chad's fault and we will get him back as soon as I can get there." Rob said. "In the meantime, Richard, you better file a report so the cops know what is going on. I'm sure they will want to question you all so get that started so when we get there it will be done." Rob instructed.

Aunt Sandra was already on the phone talking to the police and before Ericka knew it there were cops there at the house. She didn't even remember hanging up the phone with Rob. But somehow life was just moving forward like nothing was out of the ordinary. The next few hours were spent speaking to different detectives and others who were still at the house that had helped in the search. They described what Steven looked like and where they saw the blood. Ericka sent a picture of Steven to the detective so they could have it. By the time they were done with the cops it was almost dawn. Dragging herself upstairs she decided she would be no good to Steven if she was exhausted and couldn't help when the time came. She decided to grab a few hours of sleep before going to the park herself and seeing this

215

blood trail. As soon as her head hit the pillow, exhaustion claimed her.

Chapter 16

Steven moaned. His entire body hurt. He tried to get his bearings but couldn't see anything. He could feel that he was in a vehicle as he felt the bumps in the road every now and then. He just didn't know where he was going and who he was with. He also didn't know how long he had been unconscious, as all he could see was black from whatever was covering his head. He tried to move his hands and couldn't lift them. Laying there, with his head throbbing, he gingerly tried moving his head. He wanted to try and get into a more comfortable position. It was time he tried to put together what exactly had happened last night when he went to check the restrooms. He remembered hearing steps coming from behind him. He had tried to turn to see who it was but the next thing he knew he was in pain and his world had gone black. Now he found himself heading somewhere unknown with someone who was also unknown.

"I'm glad you are waking up. I was afraid I might have hit you too hard." Came a voice.

"Where am I? And what do you want?" Steven asked.

"Well, you are on your way to a meet someone and they are anxious to meet you. And as for what I want, well I wouldn't want to spoil that surprise." Came the voice.

"Are you working for Chad?" Steven asked.

"I guess in a way you could say that. But we will save the details until later. Now I want you to lay back and be quiet. We have a bit of distance to cover before we reach our destination." The voice replied.

Ok so they were leaving Lombard. That could make finding him harder for Ericka. But he was also glad they were going away from where Ericka was. Steven laid there for what seemed like hours before the vehicle started to slow down. They turned off what must have been the highway as the road they were on now was definitely bumpier than before. At one point Steven thought he might bounce off the seat. But he was able to keep his balance. They continued on for a long time, but finally they started to slow down. Stopping the car sent Steven tumbling off the seat and onto the floor boards. With his hands tied behind him, he couldn't catch himself. Laying there panting from the pain he thought of Ericka and all the pain that Chad had put her through. This was nothing in comparison to that. Taking a deep breath, he slowed his breathing. He didn't want to show weakness to whomever had taken him.

Soon the door opened and he felt hands on his shoulders pulling him out of the vehicle. Throwing Steven onto the ground the voice laughed. "I have wanted to throw a punch at you for the past week. I almost spoiled my entire plan when I saw you proposing to Annie yesterday. She is not for you. I saw your display at the ball. Kissing her in front of everyone. You were just asking for trouble." The voice said. Yesterday? That meant it was morning already. Pulling Steven up the man pulled the hood off Steven's head.

"Ricky. I should have known. I just thought you'd grab Ericka not me. Were you lying in wait for me or for her?" Steven asked.

"Does it matter really? The end result will be the same either way." He responded as he pushed Steven toward a cabin.

Stumbling Steven asked, "And what result would that be?" The more he could get Ricky to talk the greater chance he had to figure out what their end game was and how he could help Ericka.

"You don't need to worry about that. You have other things to keep your attention. Like being tied up and at my mercy." He laughed at his own joke.

Steven looked around and saw nothing but trees. Turning around he saw the cabin. This must be where Chad was hiding out. Trying to get more information out of Ricky he said, "So the coward sent you to do all the dirty work for him huh? You know you will get all the blame and Chad will get off free and clear since you were the one who kidnapped me."

"You think you have everything figured out, don't you?" Ricky asked. "Well, you are way off. But I'll save that explanation for later."

"I know you have been following Ericka and I all week, and that you harbor some feelings for Ericka, yourself. I've seen the way you look at her. She didn't think you were much of a threat though. She wrote you off as just being Chad's best friend." Replied Steven.

The punch to the stomach came quickly. With his hands bound, he couldn't protect himself. But at least now he knew he was on the right track. He must have hit a nerve about Ericka not thinking much of Ricky. But that brought up even more questions and potential issues, the main issue being Ericka truly didn't see Ricky as a threat.

Pushing Steven toward the cabin, Ricky said, "I have known Annie since she was a kid. We grew up together. She doesn't know what is best for her. But we will see about that soon enough now won't we."

"What do you mean? Chad planning something for her?" Steven asked, worried even more now since he was nowhere near Ericka to protect her.

Ricky shoved Steven, toward the cabin. "Shut up. You keep asking questions, like you have a say in what is happening. Do you not realize you are at our mercy? You are tied up and let's be honest, a little beat up too. How's your head by the way?" He asked shoving him toward the cabin again.

Once inside, Steven saw a small living space off an equally small kitchen. There were three doors off the main part of the cabin. Must be the bedrooms and bathroom. Ricky started dragging Steven toward one of the doors. Opening it up Steven saw a small bed and a dingy window. Steven had to come up with an escape plan. But what he really needed was his hands untied. "Think you might untie my hands now we are here?" Steven asked. "I need to use the restroom."

"Do you think I'm dumb? I know as soon as I turn my back you will either try to attack me or escape." Snorted Ricky. "I'll untie you while you use the bathroom but don't expect to stay that way."

Ricky grabbed Steven and drug him to the bathroom. Opening the door, he untied his hands. You have five minutes."

Steven looked around the bathroom and saw the tiny window above the shower. There was no way he would fit through that. There was a knock on the door. "This is your two-minute warning." Ricky said through the door.

Pushing escape to the back of his mind, he needed to use the facilities and get a drink from the faucet if he could. He needed to stay hydrated and who knew when the next time he would have something to drink or eat. At that thought his stomach rumbled. He didn't have time for hunger but his body had other ideas. Flushing the toilet, he washed his hands and got a couple handfuls of nasty looking water before Ricky opened the door.

"Hands." Was all Ricky said. He tied Steven's hands behind him again and drug him back to his little room. He heard noises coming from the other bedroom and wondered who else was there.

Pushing Steven onto the bed he said, "Get comfy. You're going to be here a while." And with that he turned and walked out the door, locking it behind him.

Face down on the bed, Steven took a minute just to breathe. His head and wrists were throbbing painfully. Struggling, he rolled over and tried to sit up. He needed to have a look around the room to see if there was anything he could use to cut through the bindings. Standing he went to the window first. He could barely see out through the dirt on the panes of glass. He must be at the back of the cabin as there was only trees out the window. There was only one window in the tiny room. He had hoped there might be a jagged edge somewhere around the window but found nothing. He carefully investigated the rest of the room and found nothing to assist him. Steven sat back down on the bed and tried to calm his thoughts. He was tired, sore, angry and worried. At least Ericka was safe for the time being. He laid on his side and tried to get comfortable. He needed to get some rest if he was going to try and escape at some point.

Laying on the bed, he could hear Ricky in the other room talking to someone. He heard a thud and then a loud laugh. He wasn't sure who had got hit or who was laughing but it sure sounded like he wasn't the only one in a bit of trouble. Perhaps he could use that in his favor. Maybe he could bribe the worker in trouble to help them both get out of there. Steven knew that Rob would be trying to get a hold of him if Ericka hadn't already called him right away. Ericka was safe and reinforcements would be on their way. He just needed to figure out where he was and how to get word to them. The thought of Ericka laying in his arms in their bed calmed his breathing and he was able to drift off into a fitful sleep.

Chapter 17

Ericka awoke with a start. Jemma was there shaking her shoulder. She had been trying to get Ericka awake for the past five minutes. "Ericka. It's ok, it's just me." She whispered to her friend.

"What are you doing here? I thought you were going to stay on the island?" Ericka jumped up and hugged her friend. "Where is Rob? Ericka asked.

"He is downstairs with your aunt and uncle and Mike. We decided that the best place for me was here with you and with him." She responded and hugged Ericka harder. "Besides, Steven is my brother, I want to help and Rob knew he wouldn't be able to talk me out of coming."

"Well, I don't want you to get hurt because of me, but I am really glad you are here." Pulling back from Jemma she said, "Let's go find your brother, shall we?"

They went downstairs and found everyone around the kitchen table discussing what had been done and trying to formulate a plan. Rob stood and came over and enfolded Ericka into a hug. "We will get him back. Don't you worry." He whispered into her hair.

Not trusting herself to break down and cry, she nodded and sat down next to Jemma at the table. "I didn't mean to sleep so long, what have I missed?"

"Not much actually. The police have been by once but they haven't found anything. No witnesses or leads to follow. I am glad Rob and his dad are here though, the more eyes we have the better." Responded her uncle Richard.

"Well, you can count on Ericka's and my eyes also. We are in this together." Jemma stated.

"Jem you know we discussed this on the plane. You are going to stay here with Ericka." Rob said.

"No, Rob. You told me I was staying, there was no discussion. Steven is my brother and Ericka's fiancé. We will help." Replied Jemma.

"I'm not sure..." her uncle never got to finish that statement as Ericka stood up.

"I am going to the park to look at this trail of blood and to see if I can see anything, or rather feel anything. You all forget two things," she addressed the group. "First, I have a sense that none of you, nor the police have. And second, I have lived with Chad, been abused by Chad, so I am the best pair of eyes you can have. I have seen more than I am willing to admit and I know if there are clues to be found I will find them." She turned to leave the room and felt a hand on her arm.

"You are not leaving without us." Her aunt Sandra and Jemma said together.

Smiling to herself she looked around to the men and they nodded. Gathering their things, they decided to go to where the ball was held first. There were people there cleaning up from the night before and they may have seen something in the hours since the ball had ended. Rob went and talked with a group of people and her uncle went to another group. Ericka, Jemma and her aunt all stayed together with Mike. Ericka needed to clear her head and look around. If ever there was a time she needed her special talent, it was now.

Their small group walked the perimeter of the ball area. Looking around as they went. There were a couple of men that were at the ball area but not really with the group. Ericka stopped and pretended to look around the area all the while watching these men. They looked familiar but she couldn't place them. She watched as they talked and watched Rob talking to the group of people. She could tell by their body language that they were on edge and tense. Ericka looked over to where Rob was standing and caught his eye. Ericka motioned her head toward the men. Rob raised his eye brow in question and turned slowly to look at the men. He then looked back at Ericka and with a slight nod to her, he ended his conversation and came to join their group.

"What is it?" he asked Ericka.

"I don't know. Something isn't right with them. They don't seem to be doing anything but watching people and I could swear I've seen them before but I can't place them." Ericka replied.

"That's good enough for me to at least question them, don't you think?" Rob started toward the men but Ericka stopped him with a hand on his arm.

"Wait. We don't want to spook them if they are involved." Ericka said. "Everyone needs to look at something other than them or we will scare them off. Let me talk to them. If they are involved, they will know who I am. You can be close by watching the entire thing." Ericka suggested.

"I don't know. I am not sure putting you in the direct line of fire is the smart move." Rob countered.

"They won't do anything right now, there are too many people for them to get away. All I want to do is establish if they even know Chad or Ricky." Ericka said.

"Ok but I will be close by. All you have to do is raise your voice and I will be by your side. Got it?" he asked.

"That's all I ask Rob. We need information and the only way we will get it is if I am the one asking the questions. This is the right move. I feel it." Ericka replied.

Nodding at Ericka, Rob walked over to an area close to the men and pretended to look around the ground for clues. If Ericka was right, and she usually was, they had been watching him since they got to the park. Rob watched as Ericka slowly approached the men. He really hoped he was doing the right thing here by giving her the lead in this.

Ericka slowly walked around toward the men. She didn't want to spook them. As she approached, she smiled at them. "Hello. Can I ask you a question?" she addressed the men.

They looked at each other and then back to Ericka. "Depends on the question." One of the men replied.

"Well, I was just over there with my friends, showing them the park where I grew up and I saw you both here and thought you looked familiar. Did we go to high school together by chance?" she asked them.

Shaking their heads, no, they said, "We never went to school with any Chandlers."

"Oh well. Then I must know you from somewhere else." She stated.

"No. You don't know us." One of the men said.

"Well, how did you know I was a Chandler if we don't know each other." She retorted.

The two men looked at each other and then at Ericka. They stepped toward her, "You don't want to do that," Ericka stated. "I have friends all over this park right now. You come any closer and I can guarantee they will come for you." She looked over at Rob who had stood up and was watching the exchange. He folded his arms across his chest and nodded at Ericka that he understood.

"What do you want Annie?" one asked.

"So, you do know who I am. Well, I want to know where my fiancé is." She requested

"How the hell should we know where your fiancé is? We don't even know, ugh." The other man elbowed the man talking in the stomach.

So, they were looking for someone too. "Do you know where Chad is then? I need to talk to him."

"You aren't the only one." Murmured the man rubbing his stomach.

Raising her eyebrow, she looked over at Rob. Rob started over toward the men. "We don't know where Chad or your fiancé is and that's the truth. We have been looking for Chad for days. We thought Ricky would know but he has also disappeared." The man who elbowed the other man said. He started pulling the other man toward the parking lot.

"Wait I have a few more questions." Ericka cried as the men took off toward the parking lot.

"Do you want me to chase them down?" Rob asked coming up behind her.

"Nah they don't know what's going on. And they don't know where Chad is. It sounded like they were looking for Chad or Ricky too." Ericka told Rob.

"Ok so they are having internal issues then. That doesn't help our situation." Rob said walking out from behind Ericka. "I wonder if we should still follow them. They might lead us to Ricky."

"To be honest I think that is who they are looking for. They mentioned that Ricky would know where Chad was but he disappeared too." Ericka turned to Rob. "What did you find out from that other group?"

"Not much. No one saw anything." Rob answered, rubbing his hand down his face in frustration.

"I want to look at the place where the blood was found." Ericka said.

They met up with Richard and the others and walked over to the restrooms. Richard showed everyone where the blood they found was at. Ericka walked over and looked at the ground. There were only a few splatters of blood, which was encouraging. Standing up she looked toward the restrooms. Turning slowly, she looked all around the spot she was standing at to get a lay of the land.

Everyone watched as Ericka surveyed the land. She needed to put herself in Steven's place to see if she could figure out what happened. Bending over she touched one of the blood splatters. The hair on the back of her neck stood up. She could feel something. She slowly stood and looked toward the trees. From this point there was the path on the right leading back to the dance floor, a path on the left leading to the parking lot, behind was the path to the restrooms and in front of her were just a bunch of trees. She made her way to the trees with Rob right behind her. "What is it?" Rob asked.

"I'm not sure. I just feel like there was someone in the woods. Doesn't it look like a great place to hide while waiting for someone? I think we should look around in there." Ericka said.

"Ok." Rob motioned for everyone to follow. "Ok we are going to look in the woods but we need to be careful not to disturb anything. So, watch where you are stepping. If you see anything unusual yell out for us. Jemma & Sandra you stay with me and Ericka please." Everyone else dispersed along the tree line.

Ericka started forward and looked around the bases of the trees. There was nothing. Moving further into the woods she looked at the base of the trees again, as that would be the place most disturbed. She was just about to turn back when she saw a reflection on the ground ahead of her. She bent over and saw a couple piles of leaves around what appeared to be footprints. She moved the leaves around and found a couple cigarette butts. Moving to the other pile of leaves she felt something hard and pulled up what appeared to be a key chain. "Rob, I think I found something." she called out.

Coming over he bent down and looked at the foot prints too. "It looks like someone was here for a while if those cigarettes were theirs."

Ericka nodded. "Look what else I found. It looks like it's a keychain." She handed it over to Rob and looked around the area where the foot prints were.

There was a hedgerow behind the footprints and more trees on either side. On the other side of the hedge row was a small drive way. Just big enough for one vehicle. Ericka walked over and looked at the base of the hedgerow. There was a bunch of branches but one looked broken. Picking it up she saw the wood was freshly broken and there appeared to be blood on the broken section. "Rob." Ericka gasped. Steven must have been taken here.

Rob reached out and took the branch from Ericka and looked into her eyes. "Are you ok?" he asked.

"No. But at least we found this. We need to call the detective so they can do a thorough search here. Then we need to try and figure out where the keychain came from." She took out her phone and started taking pictures. She took pictures of the footprints, where the cigarette butts were and placed the keychain back where she found it and took a picture. She also replaced the branch to where she found it so she could get a picture too. She continued to get close up shots of everything while Rob called the detective.

By the time the detective came and they went over everything they had found, it was almost sunset. They wouldn't be able to search much longer even if they had an idea where Steven was taken. They decided to head back to the Chandler's house and get some dinner and discuss everything they found today.

Chapter 18

Steven didn't want to open his eyes. He knew that if he did his dream would end. His head still hurt. Not to mention his arms were numb from being in one position for so long. Laying there with his eyes closed he tried to go back into the dream he had been having of Ericka. They were at his parent's house and they were on a walk in the woods. He smiled remembering what happened in those woods just a couple weeks ago. He was still picturing Ericka wrapped in his arm when there was a loud crash in the other room. Opening his eyes, he tried to lift his head up when there was a scream. Sitting up he sat there and watched the door. Whatever was going on in there Steven knew it would sooner or later spill over into his room and he would be in the middle of it. Just as he was able to stand up, the door burst open. "The time has come. Remember that person I told you about? Well, he is quite anxious to meet you. He is a little impatient right now." Ricky said, stepping into the room and shoving Steven toward the door.

In the main room he saw someone sitting in a chair with his hands tied to the legs of the chair. His back was to Steven so he couldn't see his face. His head was drooping down so his chin was resting on his chest. Steven saw the chair next to the man and knew that was for him. Ricky shoved him from behind. "Have a seat."

Sitting down, Ricky untied Steven's hands and tied him to the chair. The change in position drew a groan from him. He was stiff and sore from not moving his arms for hours. Steven looked over to the guy next to him. He had definitely taken a beating. And from the looks of him he had been there a while too. Some of those bruises were already turning green, meaning they were at least a week maybe two weeks old. It looked like he had a broken nose and busted lip on top of the other bruises. The man didn't even try to look at Steven.

"Where are my manners?" Ricky said. "Steven Morgan, may I introduce you to Chad Hadley. Annie Chandler's ex-husband."

Steven turned to look at Chad. *What the hell?!* If Chad was here, strapped to a chair, who the hell had been watching them? Steven looked at Ricky. "You've been the one behind this from the very beginning, haven't you?" He asked. "I knew when I first met you that there was something more going on here. You seemed too familiar with Ericka. Were you even trying to grab me or was I just convenient?"

"Ding, ding, ding, we have a winner. Although in all fairness, I have not been waiting as long as Chad has. I've only recently taken a more hands on approach. Chad really has been stalking and following Annie for years and so I just tagged along when he found out she was in LA. I went to LA with Chad to grab her and bring her back here. I was just helping him until you all got back from Oregon. But he screwed up and I got pissed. We thought it would be easier after you got back but no, you had to come with that other guy and help her. So, I took over. I saw you and that other man pack her up and thought I would have to follow you to Hawaii, but I had Chad restrained and I needed to settle him here. But then low and behold you showed up in town right on my doorstep, making my job a whole hell of a lot easier."

"But why? I don't understand?" Steven looked between Chad and Ricky. "You love her, don't you?" he asked Ricky.

"You don't have to understand. This has nothing to do with love. I may have entertained thoughts of love at some point long ago but not any longer. I'm not going to get into those details, quite yet though. You have had so many eyes on her, I couldn't get to her. You were the next best thing as, you and I both know, she will willingly give herself up to save you. Especially if she does love you like I think she does." He replied.

"No, she doesn't love him. She loves me," Cried Chad earning a whack from Ricky.

"Oh, shut up Chad. You know she doesn't love you. She stopped loving you the moment you started beating her." Ricky said.

"Ricky you aren't making sense. You say this isn't about love but I've seen the way you look at Ericka." Steven accused.

That earned him a punch to the chin. Pain shot through his head causing his already sore head to pound fiercely. "Her name is Annie." Chad yelled again.

Gingerly, Steven ran his tongue along his lip. He could taste blood, but it wasn't too bad. Ricky walked away and into the kitchen. Steven spit out blood onto the floor. He turned and saw Chad was staring at him. "What?" Steven asked.

"Did you really propose to her?" Chad asked.

"Yes, I did, and when I get out of here, I will marry her. You are an idiot. You didn't know what a good thing you had. If I wasn't strapped to this chair, I would beat you myself for the pain you have caused Ericka." Steven threatened.

"Her name isn't Ericka, it's Annie." Chad yelled at Steven. "And she won't marry you, she is already married to me. Once I dispose of him," he nodded toward Ricky, "I will take care of you. Then there will be no one to distract her from me."

"You really are delusional if you think she would just stay with you. Not to mention the fact that we are both strapped to these chairs, by someone equally are crazy as you. How do you intend to dispose of him if you are tied up?" Steven laughed. "If this wasn't such a serious problem for me, I would actually laugh at your stupidity."

Chad rocked the chair he was on and tried to throw himself at Steven, knocking himself and Steven over onto their sides in the process. Chad was yelling, "I'm going to get her back. You just watch!" He spat at Steven.

Ricky stood there watching the whole fight unfold. "I should just let you two at each other. It would save me time in the long run. But unfortunately, I need you both for this plan to work. And I don't have time for this." He walked over and grabbed Chad and sat him up straight. Untying his hands from the chair he helped him stand. It was then that Steven saw just how thin Chad was. Chad must be really

239

strung out. Which would explain his delusions. Ricky pulled Chad away from Steven and tied his hands in front of him again and shoved him into his room.

Ricky came out of the room and went into the kitchen. Steven caught a whiff of something cooking and his stomach grumbled. Steven tried to ignore the hunger pains and looked around the room. Now that Chad was gone, he could take his time and see if he could come up with a plan. There wasn't much to work with, but what caught his attention was a framed picture on the wall. It was a family with a young boy. "Do you know the people who own this cabin?" He gestured toward the picture.

"Well, aren't you full of questions. Questions that could cause you a lot of pain. So, I suggest you drop the subject, otherwise I might drop your food." He retorted.

A few minutes later he came out and righted Steven and untied him. Helping him stand he tied his arms in front of him as well and then shoved him into his room and closed the door. A few minutes later Ricky came back in with some food and a bottle of water.

"I would take your time with both the food and the water. I am leaving for a bit and you'll need to make that last." Ricky said as he closed the door and locked it.

Steven heard Ricky go into the room next door and he said the same thing to Chad. Luckily Ricky tied them up with their arms in front. He could work with his hands bound together. He took a drink and ate some of the bread. He heard the door leading into the other room close. Waiting, he listened for the front door to open and shut. The sound of the car starting and pulling away allowed Steven to take a deep breath and relax a bit. He was safe for the time being but he was worried that Ericka wasn't. She didn't know that Chad wasn't behind everything which put her at risk. He finished what food he had and slowly stood. He needed to get to work trying to break out of the room. Who knew how long Ricky would be gone? He needed to get to Ericka to protect her, now more than ever.

Chapter 19

Ericka was walking in the park with Steven. They were near the gazebo and they stopped to watch the sunset. They were wrapped in each other's arms. She felt safe and wasn't afraid of anything. There was a noise behind them and she turned to see the two men coming from the woods towards them. Steven whispered in her ear. "It's ok. I won't let anything happen to you."

"I know but what will happen to you?" She asked him.

"That's not as important right now. Right now, I need you to remember where you have seen them before. I know you recognize them. But from where Ericka? You have all the answers in your head my love. You just need to let yourself go to that place you try to keep locked away." Steven said as he started walking away from Ericka toward the two men.

"Where are you going Steven?" she yelled at him.

He turned and smiled at her. "I am going to where you will find me my love. Remember I will love you always."

The two men walked up to Steven and took him by the arms. They led him to a beat-up gray car in the parking lot. Looking at the car Ericka saw something hanging from the rearview mirror. She needed to get closer so she could see what it was. Where had she seen this car before? Getting to the car she saw the driver was Ricky. None of this was making any sense. Chad was the one who was after her not Ricky. Granted Ricky could have been the one who took Steven since he was at the ball, but it didn't make sense.

Ricky looked at her and just laughed. "You never saw it. All those years ago and even now. It has always been right there in front of you."

The door of the car closed and Ricky started to pull out of the parking lot. "You can't take him. Take me. I am the one he wants not Steven." She started running after the car trying to keep her eyes on it. She saw it get on I94 headed east.

"Wait. Don't take him." She screamed.

"Ericka." She turned and saw Jemma. "Ericka, wake up."

She woke up screaming. Jemma and Rob were both there along with her aunt and uncle. Ericka was breathless. She needed to catch her breath. She looked at Rob and

Jemma. Rob went to hug Ericka and Jemma said, "Not yet love. She needs to breathe and tell us what she saw."

Rob looked at Jemma and then back to Ericka. "What are you talking about?" He asked.

"When Ericka has dreams like this, they usually mean something." She turned back to Ericka. "Am I right? Did you see something?" She asked.

"I think so but I may need help working through all the stuff. It just kept throwing images at me." She took a breath and said, "Let's head downstairs. I'm going to need a drink."

They all shuffled downstairs and into the dining room. Aunt Sandra grabbed a bottle of whiskey and poured all who needed some a glass.

"Whenever you are ready Ericka." Jemma said, while taking her hand.

Taking a drink, she felt the burn down her throat and took a deep breath. "Steven and I were walking in the park and we came to the gazebo. The two men from today were coming toward us and Steven said I knew all the answers I just had to look deep into the places I keep hidden away. He started walking toward the men who each grabbed an arm and took him to a beat-up gray car." She heard an audible intake of breath and looked up. She locked eyes with her aunt. She continued, "The keychain I found at the park was hanging from the rearview mirror and Ricky was driving, not Chad. Ricky said that I was blind and that I never saw back then and even now. Then they pulled out of the parking lot. I tried to chase them but they got on the I94 headed east and that's when Jemma woke me up."

Ericka looked at her aunt again who was now covering her mouth with her hands. "Do you know what car I'm talking about?" She looked at her uncle who had gotten up and stood behind her aunt.

Nodding her aunt said, "The car your parents died in was an old gray car. There was a keychain hanging from the rearview mirror too."

Jemma grabbed Ericka's hand. "I don't understand why would I dream of that I don't remember them."

"Because sweet heart you were in the car when they crashed on I94. You survived, but your parents didn't." her uncle answered for her aunt.

Rob got up and came over by Ericka and knelt down. "This has to be a sign. Both the car and the highway were in your dream. Can you remember anything else about the dream?"

"Why don't I remember being in the accident?" Ericka asked her now sobbing aunt.

"You were having horrid nightmares. We didn't know what to do. We took you to a doctor who suggested hypnosis to help get you past the nightmares. After that session you didn't have any more nightmares." Her uncle said.

"Do you have a picture of the key chain from today, Ericka? I would like to see it." Her aunt whispered.

Grabbing her phone to look for the picture she had taken early that evening. She gave her phone to her aunt and her aunt nodded. "Yes, that was the one hanging from the rearview mirror."

"Ok so I think we need to go over the details of the crash. I'm sorry Ericka but we need to see how it is connected to this situation." Rob suggested.

"I completely agree Rob," replied Ericka.

Uncle Richard poured a drink for her aunt and sat down next to her. He took her hand and looked into her aunt's eyes. "You will have to bear with us, this is a particularly painful memory for us. Not just because of the wreck but the coming days afterward too." He took a drink of his whiskey and started the tale.

"Your parents had taken you to the lake to go camping. And you were so excited. On the way to the lake, there was a drunk driver who swerved and hit the car head on. Your parents were both killed instantly, and you didn't even have a scratch on you. The drunk driver survived as well as his son. The wife did not make it. We drove to the accident as quickly as we could, to get you. When we got there, you were sitting with the other boy and both of you were just holding hands, not really old enough to know what was happening but old enough to know something bad had happened."

"The drunk driver was arrested and the police handed you over to us, but the little boy got turned over to child services. You came to us right away and wrapped yourself around your uncle. And the little boy just cried and cried. We had the car scrapped and then took care of all the details of the funeral. We never saw the little boy again. The driver got life in prison for the deaths of three people while being under the influence and child endangerment."

"Ok. I have so many questions. But first, do you know the name of the driver? We can look him up and see if we can find the son." Rob said.

"Wait, if you scrapped the car, how did the key chain get to the park?" Ericka asked.

Shrugged her aunt said, "I don't know. The car was pretty smashed. There was glass and metal everywhere on the road. Perhaps if flew out of the car during the crash."

"Where were we going camping at? Do you know?" Ericka asked.

"We don't know which camp, but we know it was in Van Buren State Park. You never made it there so we didn't think it important." He uncle replied.

"What are you thinking Ericka?" Jemma asked.

"I'm not sure but I think we need to find the boy. I think he might be the key to this. I don't think the direction in my dream was an accident either. I think we need to look in the state park and see what's there." Ericka stated.

Nodding her head, Jemma said, "I was thinking the same thing."

Rob grabbed his phone and called someone, while uncle Richard said, "I think we still have a newspaper clipping. We kept a few things in case we needed to explain the situation to you. We probably should have sooner but you were already having so many problems with Chad we didn't want to add to them."

Aunt Sandra stood up and walked to the living room. There was a chest that held family keepsakes. She cleared it off and opened the lid. She dug around and brought out a photo album. She brought it to the table and took Rob's chair next to Ericka. "I think we actually have a picture of your parents in front of their car, I'll have to look for it though. This album I believe has the newspaper clipping." She opened it up and turned to a page with different newspaper articles. There were articles ranging from the grand opening of the store, to the wedding announcement of Annie and Chad. Slowly she went through the newspapers until she came to the one title,

Fatal Crash on I94 Claims Three Lives.

DUI involved fatal crash on I94 claims three lives; Mark and Connie Chandler and Sophia Adams, leaving two children, Anne Chandler, Joshua Adams and the drunk driver, named Ned Adams alive. Ned Adams has been arrested and family and family services have been contacted for the children. Traffic was stopped while emergency services worked on cleanup of the vehicles and were able to clear the roadway.

Ericka read the article, and then re-read the article. Joshua Adams. She didn't remember anyone with the last name of Adams. Maybe this wasn't the correct path after all.

She was reading the article a third time when her aunt placed her hand on her arm. "Here, I found a picture of your mom and dad in front of the car. It was before you were born but it really hadn't changed much."

She handed the picture over to Ericka who took it and gasped. It was the same car as in her dream. This was the path she was supposed to go down. She looked at the car and could see something hanging from the mirror but couldn't make it out. Ericka looked up at her aunt and took her hand. "This is not your fault. This is no one's fault other than the people who like hurting others. I am not upset with you in the slightest. You did what you thought was right and I am so glad you did. I don't know if I could have lived with those memories." She wrapped her arms around her aunt and held her while she sobbed on her shoulder.

Jemma took the picture and showed it to Rob. Ericka could feel they were getting closer. She just hoped that Steven could hang on until they could gather enough information to help him. Her aunt pulled away and wiped her eyes. Jemma turned to aunt Sandra, "Do you know how far this National Forest is from here?"

Aunt Sandra took a deep breath, "Between two and a half hours to three hours, depending on where you intend to camp. The forest has a stretch of lake that runs along it so it's very popular. A lot of the richer folks even have lake houses or cabins there. We always just went camping though."

"Were you going to be camping with us too aunt?" Ericka asked.

Aunt Sandra looked over to uncle Richard. "No, we had decided against going this time. We had just found out we were pregnant and wanted to stay home." Her aunt whispered.

"Wait, what?! I didn't know you were ever pregnant." Ericka covered her aunts' hand with her own.

"When we found out about the wreck and brought you home, we were still all in shock of losing your mom and dad. That shock took a toll on me and I lost the baby shortly after the wreck." Whispered her aunt.

"Oh aunt. I am so very sorry. This must bring up all those memories too." Ericka hugged her aunt. This time Jemma joined in the hug. Jemma had gone through a loss like her aunt so she knew the pain her aunt was dealing with.

They decided to take a break and aunt Sandra went into the kitchen to start making some food and coffee. No one was going to get anymore sleep this night. Not after all these revelations and memories surfacing again.

Ericka still wasn't sure why Ricky was driving the car in her dream and what he had meant when he said, she had never seen it. This was all about Chad, or at least that is what she thought it was all about. This new information brought up so many unanswerable questions.

She still hadn't figured out where she knew those two men from the park. But the more she thought about her dream and the new information from her aunt and uncle, she felt this was about so much more than a crazy ex who was stalking her. The fact that Ricky had been following them all around town and at the ball meant he had more to do with this and Steven's disappearance than probably Chad.

Chapter 20

Rob spent most of the morning on the phone, instructing people to search for Joshua Adams and Ricky Tucker, while Jemma and Ericka searched the web to see if they could find anything on the Adams' family. The hall of records was closed due to it being Sunday. But the longer they didn't find information the more Ericka started to worry they would be too late once they got the information.

Around lunch time they had an unexpected visitor. There was a knock at the door and aunt Sandra went to answer it. Everyone was still working when she returned with Paige and Trevor Morgan, Steven's parents. Jemma jumped up, "Mom, Dad, how are you here? I only called you last night."

"We were able to get on the first flight out of Portland." Paige said as she hugged Jemma.

Trevor walked up to Ericka, who had dropped her head. She couldn't look them in the eye. She was the cause of so much pain. Trevor lifted her chin with his finger and looked her in the eye. "This is not your fault. Please don't push us away." He wrapped his arms around her and Ericka just fell to pieces. Sobbing she just held on to Trevor. Paige joined the hug as well as Jemma, which caused even more tears to fall.

"I am so sorry. I was afraid you would hate me." She confessed.

"How could I ever hate my daughter. As a little birdie let slip that I am going to be getting another daughter soon." Trevor said and kissed the top of her head.

Paige turned Ericka around and cupped her face with her hands. "We love you Ericka and I am so happy you and Steven finally realized what we all knew. You were made for each other."

Hugging Paige, Ericka knew they couldn't wait around any longer. "Rob. I think we should drive to Van Buren National Forest. We can try the campsite that my parents were going to be camping at." Ericka explained.

"Wait, I think I might have found something." Jemma said. "Right before my parents came in, I thought where would and where could someone hide? So, I thought what about empty houses or cabins for sale. I started looking at the properties listed for sale in that area and came across this listing. It's for sale by owner, an Edward Adams." Turning to look at Ericka, Jemma said, "Wasn't the drunk driver a Ned Adams? Ned is short for Edward, isn't it? Maybe his estate is being sold off."

"You are a genius!" Ericka cried. "We need to go check this out. It's too much of a coincidence to ignore." Leaving aunt Sandra, Paige and Mike behind they loaded up and started for the Van Buren National Forest.

Uncle Richard was driving so Ericka sat with Jemma and Rob. They were about an hour into the drive when Rob got a call. "Hey what did you find out?" Rob asked. "Wait I want you to repeat that now you are on speaker." Rob said.

"It looks like Joshua Adams, was adopted and they changed his name to Richard Tucker, aka Ricky Tucker." The man on the phone said. "His biological father recently died in prison and Mr. Tucker was named the executer of his estate, otherwise I wouldn't have been able to find the information. It looks like he has some property that he has recently listed for sale. The prison records show no visits from Ricky during his father's incarceration."

"We are about an hour away from the cabin that he listed," Rob told the man. "We will keep you posted. Please keep digging. We need to know of any other places he could have taken Steven. Also, what is the status on tracking down Chad Hadley? Any news there?"

"No. It appears he has fallen off the face of the earth. We have record of him getting fired and heading to Los Angeles but after that we have lost him. We are still looking but the Joshua Adams or Ricky Tucker seems like a better trail to follow at this point. I have men working both angles and will get back to you with an update as soon as we have any changes."

Rob hung up and turned to Ericka. "Are you ok? It seems Steven was correct to worry about Ricky."

"I just don't understand. Why now. If we grew up together, he could have taken his revenge at any time. This just doesn't add up. There has to be another angle we are missing." Ericka shook her head.

"I have to agree with your assessment. Maybe the death of his father brought up these memories. Or maybe like you he didn't remember being in the accident." Jemma suggested.

"Ricky is a couple years older than I am so he would have been old enough to remember the accident unless his adopted family did similar therapy like uncle Richard and aunt Sandra used on me. But it still doesn't add up. And where the hell is Chad? He was the one tracking and searching for me, not Ricky. Ricky only came into the picture when we came to town." Ericka replied. "Between those two guys at the park looking for someone and your man not being able to find a trace of Chad, leaves me more than a little worried. I don't understand why Ricky didn't say anything all these years if he was the boy from the accident. To be honest he was always the nicest to me out of all Chad's friends." Ericka stated. "In fact, now I think of it, Ricky helped me with those two men from the park once. They had stopped Chad during one of his rages."

Ericka turned to look out the window. She needed time to figure this out but time was something they didn't have. At least now she could place those two men from the park. But why were they searching for someone if they worked with Ricky, who had been at the ball? This was just one of the many questions all this new information brought up. The longer Steven was missing the less chance of finding him. They pulled off the freeway and headed up into the park. They were going to check the cabin's address that was listed first. They decided to make a pit stop to grab some gas, just in case they had to keep searching. Pulling into the gas station, Ericka felt her neck tingling like it had in LA. Slowly she looked around but didn't see anything unusual. There was a silver car that looked familiar but no one was inside. Casually she walked over to Rob and Jemma, "We are being watched." She smiled at Rob so anyone watching would think they were just having a regular chat. "It is the same feeling I had in LA."

Rob nodded and whispered, "I want both of you in the car now. This just confirms we are on the right path."

Jemma and Ericka got in the car while Rob walked to where Trevor was standing and quietly directed him to get in the car as well. They were going to need to leave quickly. They needed to get to the cabin before whoever was watching them got there. Getting back in the car Rob asked, "Did you see anyone you recognized?"

Shaking her head, no, Ericka let out a long breath. "No but that silver car looks like one that has been parked down my aunt and uncles' street. We need to leave. If they saw us then they know we are on to them."

Richard got in at that moment and said, "The silver car over there is the same one that has been parked on our street. I think it's Ricky."

Pulling out of the gas station, uncle Richard sped off toward the address of the cabin. It was another 30 minutes before they pulled off onto the driveway.

*   *   *   *   *   *   *   *

After Steven finished eating his food, he tried the door but couldn't get it to budge. He was forced to use the window to get out but it was nailed shut. Looking around he could not find anything to break it with. He was going to have to use his hands and feet to break the window. Steven pulled the mattress over to the window and propped it against the glass. He wasn't taking any chances with his safety and the mattress would act as a shield.

He started kicking at the mattress, listening for the breaking of glass. Pulling the mattress away to check his progress, he found a couple cracks. Using that as his target he continued kicking the mattress until the glass was smashed out enough for him to climb through. Using the mattress as a slide he climbed up and out of the cabin.

He slowly made his way around the side of the house. He needed to find something to get through these ropes around his wrists. Finding a small shed to the side of the cabin, he was able to find a hand saw. Cutting the rope, he rubbed his wrists while looking around. He found some more rope along with boating equipment.

Checking outside Steven started towards the woods when he heard a car. Thinking it was Ricky he sped up until he heard his name being yelled by Ericka. He froze. She was here and so was Chad and who knows when Ricky would be back. Did he have her now?

*   *   *   *   *   *   *   *

Pulling up to the cabin, Ericka threw open the car door and started toward the cabin. "Ericka, wait." Called her uncle.

Ignoring her uncle, she ran toward the cabin just as Rob caught up to her. "Wait, at least let me go first." He tried the door and found it unlocked. Opening the door, Rob called inside. "Steven are you here?" There was no reply. Rob and Ericka slowly walked into the cabin.

"Who is there? I need help. Can you please help me?" came a voice from behind a door.

"Rob. That was Chad's voice." She whispered.

Rob turned and looked at Ericka, "Are you sure? Why would he need help?"

"I don't know but I would recognize that voice anywhere. It's Chad." Ericka confirmed.

"I really don't understand what's going on but we are going to find out. Are you ready to confront him?" Rob asked.

"Yes. We need to be quick. If that was Ricky's car, he was right behind us. Maybe Steven got away and locked Chad in there while Ricky was gone." It was the only thing that made sense to Ericka.

"If that's the case Steven could be on foot in the woods." Rob said, walking to the door that Chad was behind.

Rob tried the door but it was locked. "Who's there?" Chad cried. "Whoever you are, please help me. I don't know when he will be back."

Rob kicked at the door. It took a few tries but he finally was able to get the door opened. What they saw Ericka couldn't believe. It was Chad, who was tied up and he looked like hell. He was skinny and the bruising on his body looked to be at several different stages of the healing process. "Chad?" Ericka whispered. "What the hell is going on?"

"Annie! I knew you would come for me. I told them I would get out of this and find you. Come untie me sweetheart." Chad said.

"No. I am not your sweet anything Chad. And what do you mean them? Are there more people here? You are the only one we have seen." Ericka replied.

"You are definitely mine. I told the guy who said he proposed to you that you would never marry anyone else, you were already married." Chad replied. "Now come untie me so we can get out of here."

"Steven is here?" She asked. "Where is he Chad."

"He was locked in the room next to mine." Replied Chad.

Ericka turned on her heels and ran to the other door. She tried it and it opened into a bathroom. She moved on to the other door but it was locked. Pounding on the door she yelled, "Steven. Steven are you in there?"

There was no answer. Rob came up behind her and moved her away from the door. He kicked the door a couple times before it gave way. Walking in they saw a window had been smashed. Running to the window, she stuck her head out looking both ways and saw nothing. "He must have gotten out. We need to look in the woods." Ericka said.

Turning around she saw Chad coming toward her. Rob stepped in front of her and blocked her from him. "Get out of my way," cried Chad.

*   *   *   *   *   *   *   *

Slowly Steven started back tracking. He saw his dad, Richard and Jemma by Richard's car. He was just about to make his presence known when he heard a second car pull up, but stopping further up the drive way. Watching the car, he heard a scream come from the house. He was tempted just to burst through the door but he watched as Ricky got out of his car and was sneaking toward the cabin.

*   *   *   *   *   *   *   *

Stepping around Rob, she placed a hand on Rob's arm. "Let me handle this." Rob looked between the two of them as Ericka walked up to Chad who was still tied and planted a facer hard enough to rebreak his nose. Blood went everywhere and Chad screamed.

"Well done." Rob said. "Too bad I broke the doors otherwise we could just leave him here." Rob walked over to Chad and pulled him toward the cabin door. Jemma, Trevor and Richard were all coming to the house after that scream. Trevor had a hold of Jemma and Richard was walking toward Ericka when she felt her neck tingle. She stopped, causing Rob and Chad to stop. "What is it?" Rob asked.

*   *   *   *   *   *   *   *

Steven watched as everyone came out of the cabin. Seeing the blood pouring from Chad, he smiled. Ericka paused and turned and looked right at Steven. But he didn't think she actually saw him. She turned to Rob and whispered something and then whispered to Jemma and Richard, who

263

were protesting whatever crazy scheme she had come up with.

*   *   *   *   *   *   *   *

"He is here. I feel it." Ericka turned and slowly looked toward the forest. "He is watching us."

Rob walked Chad over to car and tied him to the car door. On his way back to Ericka, he asked, "How do you want to handle this?"

"Trust me ok." She whispered to Rob. "Get Chad into the cabin and tie him up. Grab Jemma, Trevor and uncle and go into the cabin. I need to call him out. We need to finish this, Rob."

Shaking his head, "Ericka, I can't leave you to face him alone."

Smiling to Rob she said, "I'm not alone. You will be inside and I don't think I'm alone out here either." She whispered.

"Steven," he said quietly. She nodded her head. "Ok, but the first sign of trouble, we are coming out. Understood?!" She agreed and went to Jemma and Trevor who both wanted to fight her but ended up giving in.

*   *   *   *   *   *   *   *

Keeping his eyes on Ricky he saw that he had stopped and was watching Ericka. Steven turned and saw everyone including Chad and Rob go into the cabin, leaving Ericka alone. What the hell?

Looking around he needed to find something he could use as a weapon. He reached down and grabbed a big branch. He had to try and get closer without letting Ricky know he was there. If he could come up behind him while Ericka distracted him, he could take him down. Foolish, stubborn woman! That was her plan. She knew he was there and he wouldn't let her do this alone. If he wasn't so worried about her, he would have been proud.

*　　*　　*　　*　　*　　*　　*　　*

Once they were inside, Ericka moved in front of the door. "Ok Ricky, or should I say Joshua. We are alone. Let's talk. Obviously, you wanted my attention by taking Steven."

"Oh, he wasn't my original target." Ricky's voice came from the left of the cabin. "I was trying for you but everyone had you protected."

She heard footsteps in the woods to the left. "Well, I'm here now. You were in LA with Chad, weren't you? I had the same feeling there as I do now." She called out.

"Yes, I was with that idiot. He could have grabbed you before all those people arrived but didn't. After our road trip to Oregon, I decided if I wanted it done right, I had to do it myself. I had hoped that I could have Chad do all the dirty work but he got too strung out on whatever drug he was using." Came Ricky's voice from somewhere in front of Ericka. He was moving.

"Are you afraid to face me? Is that why you are hiding in the woods?" She asked trying to provoke him enough to show his face.

"I am not scared of little Annie Chandler." Ricky said as he stepped out from behind a tree.

Ericka saw something move to the right of her but never took her eyes off Ricky. She needed to distract him, "Why now Ricky? That's the part I just don't understand. You've known I was the girl from the crash the whole time, didn't you?" She asked him.

"Yes, I did." He replied. "I kept an eye on you for years. I knew the crash wasn't your fault, that my drunk dad was at fault. But when my dad died in prison not long ago, I found out that there was an inheritance and he left it to both his beneficiaries; me and you." He moved a little closer.

"This is all about money? Did you think to ask me if I wanted this money? I would have turned it over to you. I don't care about the money. I just want my life back with Steven as my partner." Ericka shook her head. "What was your plan? Kidnap Steven to force me to sign everything over or did you plan on killing me?" she asked.

"I wasn't going to kill you. I was going to leave that up to Chad. I knew if he got his hands on you again you wouldn't make it out alive. This way I got the best of both worlds, the policies to me and my hands clean of your death. Then that idiot had to screw up. I had to bring Chad back here to figure out how to track you since you moved all your stuff." He laughed to himself, "But then there you were with that other guy. You showed up here just where I needed you. I just couldn't get you alone. That guy wouldn't leave you alone for five minutes. So, I had to change my plan up."

"What is your plan now? You have several more witnesses, not to mention Chad's kidnapping. Where did you put Steven?" She asked.

"If he was not in the cabin, I don't know where he is. Lucky him." Ricky said while stepping a bit closer.

Ericka saw movement behind Ricky but kept her eyes on Ricky. She had to keep him distracted so Steven could come up from behind him. "Well, I'm not sure exactly how

267

you plan to get out of this. One word from me and my friends and family will be out here, not to the mention the family I have at home that are waiting for our call so the police know where to go."

"Well maybe I'll just grab you and we can escape together. You away from Chad, and me away from the police. You are good at hiding. It took us years to find you after New York. We could disappear together." He stepped closer

Ericka kept him talking, spilling all his plans to her while Steven snuck around and got behind Ricky. When Ricky asked Ericka to run and hide with him, Steven knew this was about more than money. Steven locked eyes with Ericka and he nodded he was ready.

Ericka said, "I don't think so. I am done running and I am not going anywhere without my fiancé. Right Steven?"

Ricky turned just as Steven swung the branch he had found, sending Ricky sprawling on the ground. "Ericka, get in the house." Rob said from behind her.

"No. I am not hiding. I am done hiding." She said as she ran over to where Steven was tying Ricky's hands together. He finished just in time to catch Ericka as she launched herself at him. Stumbling he laughed while Ericka tried to kiss every inch of his face. "Steven." She whispered.

"My love," he whispered back. "You know you took at least 10 years off my life by pulling this stunt." He said while kissing her face.

"I knew you were watching, so I knew I was safe." She said lovingly.

"You mean to tell me your neck tingled so you knew I was there?" he asked cupping her face.

"No, my neck tingled because I felt Ricky." She said, "I knew you were out there because I could feel the heat from your eyes undressing me."

"Of course, you did." He said and kissed her deeply. "You might need to fill me in though. I was so worried about getting to you I wasn't really paying attention to what you were talking about. How did you find me?" he asked.

"I had a dream that led us to you in a roundabout way." She said, kissing him again.

"Let's get him inside with Chad. Your dad has already called the police and they are on their way." Rob said. "By the way, you look like crap." He grabbed Steven and gave him a hug. "It is good to see you in one piece though."

"Steven," came a cry from the door. Jemma ran out and hugged him. "I am so glad you are ok." Jemma looked him over, "You are ok, right?"

Laughing Rob and Steven picked up Ricky and took him inside and planted him in the chair that Steven had occupied earlier that day. Trevor grabbed Steven and gave him a long hug. And even uncle Richard hugged Steven.

Ericka couldn't stop touching Steven. She wouldn't leave his side, which was driving Chad absolutely crazy. "Annie get your hands off him. And you get your hands off her." He kept yelling so they decided to put him in the room he had been in. The door was open but at least he complaints and rants were a little quieter that way.

Steven was still really sore but he was so happy to have Ericka in his arms again. They went and sat in the car so they could be alone while they waited for the police to arrive. Sitting in the car, all Ericka wanted to do was get as close as she could. She kissed his neck and gingerly kissed his bruise and split lip. "I am so sorry you got hurt because of me." She said and buried her face in his neck.

"Hey, none of that. This was not your fault." He cupped her face. "I am just glad it was me and not you that he took. Who knows what would have happened?" He kissed her gently.

Ericka looked into his eyes and wrapped her arms around him. "I'm never letting you of my sight again, Mr. Morgan." She whispered in his ear.

Steven pulled her onto his lap and kissed her. "I am good with that Miss Taylor." He whispered in her ear.

Ericka kissed his neck and ran her hands up his arms to the back of his head. Pausing Steven said, "Careful I have a nasty bump back there."

Ericka cupped his face and looked into his eyes. "Did I hurt you?" she asked.

"No. I just wanted to make sure you knew." He kissed her quickly and said, "You are more than welcome to keep seducing me though. I won't object."

Laughing Ericka said, "Oh, I'm doing the seducing huh?"

"Well, if you don't know, maybe I should remind you." He said and pulled Ericka closer. Sliding his hands down her arms he reached behind her and grabbed her bottom and pulled her closer to his erection.

"This is what you do to me, my love." He said and rubbed her against him drawing a gasp from her.

"Steven, you may want to rethink this because I may not want you to stop." She said while kissing his neck. She made her way up his neck to his ear lobe and nibbled. Making him moan.

"Steven" she whimpered.

He lifted her up and straddled him. "Christ, Ericka I need inside you."

He unbuttoned her jeans and pulled them down. "Get one leg out." He instructed. She pulled her leg out and started unbuttoning his pants. Freeing his erection, she wrapped her hand around him, causing him to groan. "I need you now love." He begged.

Getting up on her knees, she guided him to her core. As she slid down, they both moaned. Steven grabbed her face and kissed her. "I love you." He whispered.

Ericka set the pace. This was not a slow and gentle ride, she wanted to claim him for herself. She needed him just as much as he needed her. They had both been scared for the other one and being reunited brought to the surface all their fears of losing the other.

"Oh Christ, Ericka, I'm not going to last long. Come for me my love." He reached down between them and found her nub, sending bolts of pleasure through her core.

"Steven," she moaned. "Don't ever leave me again." She had her hands on his shoulders giving her leverage to increase the depth and power of each thrust.

"That's right. I am yours and you are mine." He groaned as she sped up the pace, "Ride me love, take all of me." He found her nub one more time causing her to shatter. He moaned and followed her into bliss.

Ericka collapsed on Steven and they just laid there trying to catch her breath. She lifted her head and giggled when she saw the look on Steven's face. His head was thrown back on the head rest in the car and he had the biggest smile across his face. He opened his eyes and looked at her, "Miss Taylor you know what those giggles do to me and I don't think we have time for another ride." He kissed her forehead and then the end of her nose before gently kissing her.

They froze as they heard the cabin door open and close. "Crap. I don't have my pants on." Ericka laughed.

Steven lifted her and did up his pants and moved her over to the other side of the seat. I'll distract them and give you time," he motioned toward her pants. Planting another quick kiss, he opened the door and got out laughing the entire time.

Laughing, Ericka had to fix the pant leg. She was able to get it righted and her leg inside just as her door opened. Falling backwards, Jemma caught her. "I knew it!" she was laughing and Ericka was looking up at Jemma from the seat. "When you both didn't come back in, we had a feeling you might be comforting each other."

Ericka sat up and zipped up her jeans. "Then why the hell did you open the door? I could have been naked."

"Nah you didn't have enough time for that." Jemma retorted. "Everyone wants to talk to Steven. I figured it would be better if I came out with Rob to get him instead of your uncle."

"Yes, well thank you for that. Where is Rob?" Ericka asked.

"He pulled Steven into the cabin to give you privacy and time to right any clothing." She replied.

They slowly headed toward the cabin just as a police car was pulling up the drive. They spent the next few hours dealing with the police, writing statements and handing over Chad and Ricky. Soon they were able to get underway and head back to Lombard. It was a long drive and poor Steven was exhausted and slept the entire trip with his head in Ericka's lap.

When they pulled up to the Chandler's house, Paige came running out. Ericka and Steven got out of the car and instantly Paige had her arms wrapped around Steven. She was crying and was murmuring something that Ericka couldn't make out. They all made their way into the house and was guided to the couch. Everyone was exhausted from not sleeping the previous night and all the traveling. Slowly everyone made their way to bed. With her head on Steven's chest, Ericka and Steven both fell asleep instantly.

Chapter 21

The next morning, as the sun rose, they made love slowly and tenderly. They worshipped each other like it could be their last time. There was an unspoken agreement that they were not going to take the time they had for granted. Collapsing on Steven's chest, they both were breathless and enjoying the last waves of pleasure. Lifting her head, she looked into Steven's face and giggled.

"Ugh you can't do that. I need time to recover." Steven said. This made both of them burst out laughing. Steven rolled her onto her back and looked into her eyes. "Marry me."

"I already said I would marry you. Did you forget in all the excitement?" She giggled again.

Kissing her neck just below her ear, he said, "No I didn't forget." He said kissing down to her collarbone and to the valley between her breasts. "I mean marry me today."

"Wait? What?" She tried to pull his head up so she could look him in the eye, but he had found her nipple and was distracting her. "You can't do that and carry on a conversation like this at the same time." Moaning she ran her fingers through his hair.

There was a knock on the door and Rob said, "Why do I always have to knock on their door?" He asked.

Jemma laughed, "You lost remember? Or was it won?"

"Steven you are wanted downstairs. There is a detective here that needs to talk about Ricky and Chad." Rob replied. He must have turned to Jemma and said, "Ok I want my prize." And they heard Jemma laughing while moving down the hall.

Ericka and Steven looked at each other and burst out laughing too. They got up and got dressed. Heading down the hall they could hear Jemma laughing in their room. Steven looked at Ericka and said, "I should knock on their door." Making Ericka laugh.

"Nah they don't have any kids here. Let them have some alone time. They earned it after all." Ericka said.

As they made their way down the stairs, Steven paused and turned to Ericka. "I was serious earlier. I don't want to wait to marry you. I will of course if you'd like a big wedding." He kissed her then said, "Just think about it ok?" Ericka nodded and they continued down to the dining room, which had been overtaken by the group with maps, papers, laptops and anything else they had used to try and find Steven.

They saw the detective seated with a cup of coffee in hand. "Good morning officer. How can we help you?" Ericka asked.

"We got your reports from yesterday, but we wanted to let you know of the developments that have happened since. Chad Hadley is dead." The detective said.

At this news Ericka's knees gave out. Had Steven not been right there she would have collapsed to the floor. "Ericka." Cried her aunt.

Steven picked her up and carried her to the couch in the living room. He heard his dad "Let's continue this in the living room, shall we? We have all had a trying few days."

Jemma and a very disheveled Rob came running down the stairs. "What's going on? We heard someone yell." Jemma said. Catching sight of Steven carrying Ericka to the couch, she followed him as he sat down with Ericka on his lap, Jemma sat down next to him. "What's going on?" she asked again.

"They just told us Chad is dead." Steven said. Rob came over and sat next to Jemma as the rest of the group came in from the dining room.

"I'm sorry. I didn't think the news would be taken badly after everything that happened." The detective said.

Steven nodded and rubbed Ericka's back. "We have been through a lot these past weeks not to mention years of Ericka hiding from him. It's just a lot to take in."

Nodding her agreement, she asked, "What happened? How did he die?"

"That's where things get a bit more complicated. Ricky Tucker and Chad Hadley were in the same holding cell while they were being processed. Mr. Hadley had been carrying on, about his wife Annie, since he had been transported and it appears Mr. Tucker had just reached his limits and took matters into his own hands. Fortunately for us, but unfortunately for Mr. Tucker, the cell video camera recorded the entire thing. Mr. Tucker will now be held for kidnapping, and murder."

Ericka laid her head on Steven's shoulder. He leaned down and kissed the top of her head. "Are you ok?" he whispered. Jemma picked up Ericka's hand and squeezed it.

"I think I am in shock. I have been running from him for years and now he is just gone. I actually don't know how I'm supposed to feel about this. Happy, sad, relieved? Someone please tell me what to say and do." She turned her face into Steven's chest. He pulled her closer and she breathed him in. She was safe, and Steven was safe. That's all that matters. She heard the other voices in the room and knew that uncle Richard and Trevor were handling the detective. She heard the door close and realized that the detective must have left. Steven gently lifted her chin and wiped her cheeks. She hadn't even realized she was crying. "I don't know why I'm crying." She confessed.

"No matter what has happened, he was still an important part of your life. Of course, you are going to grieve for that Chad. Not the one he turned into but the one you fell in love with. I just want to make sure you are ok." Steven said.

"I'm not sure how I'm feeling but I just need you to hold me." Ericka said.

"No problem. I'm not going anywhere." Steven said and kissed her temple.

Jemma and Rob went into the dining room to grab lunch and Steven continued to hold Ericka on his lap. They talked every now and then but just held each other. After

280

lunch, Ericka said, "Let's go for a walk." They left and headed to the park and to her tree. They weren't the only ones out on that gorgeous day and it was just what Ericka needed to lift her spirits. They sat down on a bench by her tree and watched the people in the park.

"I don't want to wait, but I don't think we should marry today. I think we should give Grant and Cindy the chance to come if they want. But after the news this morning I don't want a huge wedding or to wait a long time. I am not going to take for granted my time with you Steven. I love you." Ericka said.

Steven twined their fingers together and said, "That sounds like a good compromise. How about Saturday? We can get all the paperwork in that time and Grant and Cindy can fly here this week."

"Should we go tell everyone?" she asked.

"In a bit. I just want to sit here with you and soak in the sun." Steven replied. And they did just that.

They eventually made their way back to the house and shared the news with everyone and Steven called Grant and told him what was happening and to reassure his brother that he was home and ok. Ericka was a little worried that Jemma and Rob would have to leave to get back to the kids, but Jemma reassured her she wasn't going anywhere. Charles and Agnes were holding down the fort with the help of Molly.

The week leading up to the wedding flew by. Between getting the license, a dress and securing a few decorations and refreshments, they were kept busy. During this time, the detective informed them that Chad was going to be buried on Thursday. As much as she didn't want to go, she knew she needed to honor the man she had fallen in love with. Steven, Ericka, Jemma and Rob all attended the funeral. As Ericka placed a flower on his casket, she felt freed. She felt lighter and happier than she had been in a long time. It was just the closure she needed before taking the next step.

Before they knew it, Saturday rolled around and Ericka was excited, nervous and happy. They held the ceremony in the back yard of her aunt and uncles' house. Cindy and Jemma both stood up with Ericka as did Rob and Grant. Uncle Richard walked Ericka up to Steven and kissed her cheek and shook Steven's hand.

They decided to say their own vows to each other. Steven took both Ericka's hands in his and said, "I take you Ericka Taylor, and Annie Chandler, to be my lover, my partner, the mother of my children and my best friend. I will love you and comfort you in times of trial and in times of joy. I will support you and care for you in sickness and health. I will love you from now until the end of times. With this ring I promise to be your faithful partner."

Sliding the ring onto her finger he lifted her hand and kissed the ring on her finger. The pastor turned to Ericka. "Steven. I should have gone first because now I'm crying." She whispered getting a laugh from her brothers in law.

Taking a deep breath she vowed, "I take thee Steven Morgan to be my partner, my lover, the father of my children and above all else my best friend. I will support you and love you through thick and thin, sickness and health. I give all my love and life to you for safe keeping. You have my heart and I have yours. We will be partners in all things and love each other unconditionally. I promise to come to you with my worries and fears and I will take your worries and fears upon myself. Our souls have reunited and will always find each other in this life and the next. With this ring I promise to be your faithful and loving partner from now until the ends of time." She slid the ring onto Steven's finger and smiled up at his beaming face.

"With the exchanging of vows and rings, I can now pronounce you husband and wife. You may now kiss the bride." The pastor finished.

Steven gathered Ericka in his arms and kissed her long and deep. Rob coughed "hey now." bringing them back to the gathering of people. Steven looked at Rob and said, "You should talk." Steven smiled at Rob and Grant and embraced each of his brothers. He turned back to Ericka who was hugging Jemma. "Mind if I borrow my bride sis?"

Laughing they both turned to Steven. He kissed Jemma's and Cindy's cheeks. "I guess, if you insist." Replied Jemma.

Taking Ericka's hand, he led her back to their family and as they were passed from family member to family member, he watched as Ericka laughed, talked and truly enjoyed herself. He was so happy and he couldn't wait to sneak her out of the house. Rob and Grant had enjoyed teasing him and placed bets to see if they actually made it out of their room. He couldn't wait to give her his wedding present. But he had to make it through the luncheon first. He made his way back over to his bride and led her into the house.

"Wait, before you head inside," Jemma said, "We have a little surprise for you both."

Steven and Ericka looked at each other and shrugged. Jemma and Rob pulled them through the house and out the front door. "Where are we going?" Ericka asked.

"Close your eyes and trust us." Rob said.

Hand in hand they were led further away from the house. Before long Ericka could smell the familiar blooms of the park. "Jemma what did you do?"

"Shush and behave." Jemma said. "We are almost there."

Stopping, Jemma and Rob said, "Don't open your eyes quite yet. We have a couple things to finish."

Steven pulled Ericka into his arms and whispered, "They are cutting into our honeymoon time you know."

Laughing Jemma, smacked Steven's arm. "You hush. You are the one who gave us the idea after all, so it's your own fault."

A few minutes later, Rob stood in front of them and said, "Ok on the count of three you can open your eyes."

"One, two, three," a crowd of people yelled.

Startled, Ericka pulled Steven closer and opened her eyes. They were at the park by her spot and they had tables set up and there were lots of friends and family all seated and ready for the luncheon. "Oh, my goodness, it looks beautiful!!" Ericka cried. "Thank you so much." She wrapped her arms around Jemma and then kissed Rob's cheek.

They sat down and enjoyed a lovely luncheon. Later that evening they made their way toward the hotel. Or so Ericka thought. Pulling up in front of her uncle's store, Steven stopped and turned off the car. "What's going on?" she asked.

"I have a wedding gift for you." Steven replied.

"What could you have here?" She asked looking out the window.

She turned back to Steven and saw he was holding a key. She looked at him and raised an eyebrow. "It was too big to wrap." He said, "And it just became finalized last night. We had to rush it so it would be finished."

"I still don't understand." She questioned.

"I bought the store from your uncle. They are still going to run it for us until we are ready but I think I found my next venture." He said smiling.

"You? What?" she stammered. "Does that mean we are staying here?" she asked?

"Until we find our next adventure, it sure does." Steve replied. "And about that hotel suite, I hope you won't be too disappointed but I found us other accommodations."

"What now?" She laughed. "I may have reached my surprise limit."

"Well, you know that the store belonged to your uncle, but did you know he owned the entire block?" He asked.

"No, I had no idea." Did you buy the whole block?"

"No but there are several renovated lofts above the stores. I bought the one above the store. So now we have our own place." He whispered.

Opening the car door, he came around the car to Ericka's side and helped her out. He grabbed their bag and led her to the door to their loft. Steven unlocked the door and scooped Ericka up and carried her across the threshold. He carried her up the stairs and into the living room, where he set Ericka down. "You can make any changes you want and when we are ready for a house, we can rent it out."

Ericka slowly walked around the loft and turned to Steven, "I love it. And I love you. Thank you for doing this. I have waited a long time to come home. I am so thankful you don't mind staying here."

She walked over to Steven and wrapped her arms around him. He smiled and looked into her face, "I don't care where we are as long as we are together."

He lifted her and carried her to the bed. "I have waited all day to get you out of that dress and worship you. It's a beautiful dress by the way, but not as beautiful as your bare skin."

Smiling she knew they would be fine where ever and whatever they did, because they would do it together. They were on to their next grand adventure. They then proceeded to worship every inch of each other's body.

THANK YOU

Thank you for reading ERICKA! Please take a moment to leave a review of this book. I sincerely hope you enjoyed Ericka and Steven's story. If you would like to learn more about Jemma and Rob's story, *JEMMA* is available in paperback or eBook format. If you are a Kindle Unlimited subscriber *JEMMA* is free to download.

If you'd like to stay up to date on Tam's latest releases, future books and recommendations of other amazing authors be sure to subscribe to Tam's Romance Adventures Newsletter! www.tamscorner.com.

Turn the page to read and excerpt of Jemma and Rob's story in the first book in the *Starting Over with Love series*: *JEMMA.*

SNEAK PEEK

JEMMA

Jemma had been in Los Angeles for just over a year and had almost completed her last year of college. All she needed was 3 credits and she was done. She had been contemplating what her next move would be when Professor Williams, her instructor for her Hawaiian Culture class, approached her regarding an outreach program that was 3 credits. It was also considered a lab class since you actually had to go to Hawaii. He explained that the University had rented a campground on the big island near Hilo, Hawaii and they were going to be having a class to learn about their culture first hand. When the Professor had heard about the class, he had thought of her immediately.

It had been a week since Professor Williams had approached her. She had done some research online and found that Honomu, HI was a quaint little town and was once the hub for the sugar workers along the Hamakua Coast. It was once a bustling center for the sugar industry, with saloons, a hotel/bordello, stores, and several churches. It was about 10-12 miles north of Hilo, Hawaii.

Upon learning about the class, Jemma had called and talked to her mom to get her opinion. Jemma and her mom, Paige, had always been close. Paige was a stay-at-home mom and had always put her children first. Paige and Trevor Morgan outside of Portland, Oregon, which is a small town near the border of California and Oregon. Jemma had grown up there with two brothers Grant and Steven. Jemma being the youngest and only daughter, her brothers were very protective. Grant was married to Cindy, who Jemma considered a sister. Steven on the other hand was still single. Both of her brothers lived in Oregon. They were a close family and Jemma's mom had just visited a couple weeks ago. Mom was very encouraging about the trip and told her to go for it and they would help her out for the semester. That was all Jemma needed to hear. She had always wanted to go to Hawaii after listening to the stories of her parents' honeymoon. She had been yearning for a change and this seemed the perfect opportunity. She felt like she was floundering and didn't know where or what she wanted to do with her life. Life had changed so much in the last two years that the decisions she had made back then weren't possible any longer. It's interesting what goes through your mind when having to make life decisions after planning for something completely different.

Two years ago, she had been married and ready to embark on a life with Clint Harding and create a loving home for their family. That seemed to have been a pipe dream however, for not even three months later their marriage was over and Jemma was faced with being homeless, jobless and all alone. You tend to do a lot of soul searching when you have nothing. Luckily, she had her family who helped her get through that difficult period in her life.

It was the thought of packing up and leaving her world behind that appealed to Jemma the most about this trip, even if it was only for 3-4 months. She had been going through the motions for the past year or so, and she needed to get out of her rut. And with determination she set off to get everything in order so she could make the journey. She gave her two weeks' notice at her job, which if there was another deciding factor in her decision to go to Hawaii, it would have been quitting her job. She was happy to be able to turn in her notice and felt exhilarated as she pulled out of the parking lot her last day knowing she wouldn't have to ever come back.

Her roommates on the other hand were harder to convince. Ericka and Sally were great roommates and Jemma had been extremely lucky to have met them. Ericka was like a mother hen and had an uncanny ability to read emotions. She always seemed to know what was going to happen before anyone else. Ericka had met Sally her first day of college. All three were looking for a place to stay and decided to move in together. Sally was loud and fun. She was always out doing something with her friends. Jemma would miss both her roommates but her parents had paid for her expenses while she was gone, so at least she knew she would have a roof over her head when she returned.

Jemma had just hung up with her travel agent confirming the flight when Ericka came into the room. Jemma had been packing her things all morning and her room was a mess. She couldn't decide on what to take so it was taking longer than she had thought to get ready for tomorrow's flight. Ericka was lounging on Jemma's bed eating a bag of chips talking to Jemma as she scrambled about her room. Ericka was still trying to convince Jemma not to leave. She kept saying, "I'm never going to see you again. I know it." Jemma turned to her and smiled and said, "It's only for a semester and I'll be back before you know it."

Ericka smiled and said "Well at least I have an excuse for going to Hawaii now." She sat up and asked, "Do you need any help?"

Jemma smiled and said, "Nah, I am just deciding on which outfits to take." Ericka got up from the bed, "Well you're paid up through the semester, so you have a room to come home to. Don't have too much fun without us. Sally would never let you hear the end of it." And with that she gave her a quick hug and left.

Jemma was happy to be alone. It seemed that since she had made the decision to do this class, everyone around her seemed on edge. It really wasn't that big of a deal she told herself. It was a great class on learning more about Hawaii. This had always been something Jemma had wanted to do. Go to Hawaii and learn about their culture. And what better way to get school credits towards her degree.

There really wasn't much keeping her here in Los Angeles anymore and starting out fresh appealed to her now more than ever. She assumed she would be able to find part time work once she got there but the thought of just enjoying herself out weighed her worries about money. Yesterday was her last day at work so she had her last check to live off of and since the room and board was included in the price of the class that's really all she would need. She gathered her remaining outfits and finished packing. No turning back now, she grinned to herself. She got undressed and into bed anxious for the morning to come. Tomorrow will be the beginning of a great adventure and she was ready for whatever came her way.

Also by Tamara Eastlick

Starting Over with Love Series: Three Books

Jemma

Ericka

Coming Soon!!

Cindy

About the Author

Years before she was a mom of three, two of which are twins, Tam loved creating stories, characters and places to escape too. During a dark period of her life, she decided to get some of those stories down on paper. Writing really helped her come through that dark period. Now she is ready to share her stories with you! She believes that the heroines of the story are strong and resilient.

Tam makes her home in southern California where she spends her time writing, while being a momma. She writes steamy, contemporary and historical romances with the occasional paranormal romance.

If you'd like to stay up to date on Tam's latest releases, future books and recommendations of other amazing authors be sure to subscribe to Tam's Romance Adventures Newsletter! www.tamscorner.com.